REVENGE OF THE
VAMPIRATES

At that moment lightning streaked from the sky, illuminating a terrifying scene. The wind was howling all around, tearing at the ship's sails and whipping up the sea into a boiling, seething rage. Waves were hurling themselves at the ship. High above the fruitbats' heads the skull and crossbones of the Jolly Roger swayed and rippled as if it was performing a macabre dance. In front of the trio loomed a familiar face. Fangs glistening and skull tattoos glinting under each wing, Captain Blood had the fruitbats right where he wanted them.

Look out for:
Attack of the Vampirates

Hippo Adventure

REVENGE OF THE VAMPIRATES

Martin Oliver

Scholastic Children's Books
7–9 Pratt Street, London NW1 0AE, UK
a division of Scholastic Publications Ltd
London ~ New York ~ Toronto ~ Sydney ~ Auckland

First published by Scholastic Publications Ltd, 1995

Text copyright © Martin Oliver, 1995

ISBN 0 590 55935 4

All rights reserved

Typeset by TW Typesetting, Midsomer Norton, Avon

Printed by Cox & Wyman Ltd, Reading, Berks.

10 9 8 7 6 5 4 3 2 1

For Andrea

Chapter 1

"ATTENTION… All right, you 'orrible bunch. Get yourselves ready… Step forward for inspection."

A rustling of leaves at the top of a tall tree accompanied the orders. In the pale moonlight four small shapes could be seen hanging from various branches. The sun had dipped below the sea and night had fallen on Fruit Isle – time for a meeting of the Fruit Gang. The gang had been Ace's idea, and he never let the other members forget it. While Ace tapped his foot impatiently, two of the fruitbats whispered to each other.

"All this discipline and drilling is a bit much – even for Ace. I think he's going bonkers."

"He's gone totally batty if you ask me," the other one replied. "He needs to hang loose."

"Silence in the ranks," Ace said. "Let's have a look at you then. Who's going to be first?"

A chunky fruitbat landed heavily beside Ace. Once the tree had stopped shaking, Ace's eagle eyes checked over Rocket, the biggest member of the gang. In contrast to Ace's gleaming goggles, smart silk scarf and flying hat, Rocket's clothes were covered in bits of peel and fruit skin – the remains of his last meal – and his pockets were bulging with emergency snacks.

"You're an absolute disgrace," Ace began, pointing to a large raspberry juice stain on his jumper. "Look at this. Have you got anything to say?"

"Yes," Rocket grinned, still munching. "It was delicious."

2

Ace sighed. There was nothing he could do about Rocket. He was too big to push around and he didn't want to risk a blast of his rocket-powered, fruit-pip-spitting ability. "Next one."

Swoop glided down and landed perfectly beside Ace. Swoop was a superb flyer and the island's aerobatic champion. As usual he was wearing his sky surfer's gear of baggy shorts and baseball boots although he had turned his hat the right way round.

"You'll do," Ace muttered, finding nothing to complain about. "Still," he thought, rubbing his hands with glee. "That leaves Radar. He normally manages to get some-thing wrong. I wonder what it'll be today."

He didn't have to wait too long to find out. The smallest fruitbat in the gang landed un-steadily on the branch beside Ace.

"So what's this, then?" Ace asked, pointing to a glaring, multi-coloured scarf wrapped around Radar's neck. "This isn't standard uniform, is it? Why are you wearing it?"

3

Radar sniffed – he was going down with flu. He was about to answer Ace's question when he felt his nose twitching and a roaring noise filled his head. Oh, no, he thought as Ace moved closer. I'm going to … ahh … I'm going to… "ATTISCHOOO!"

At the last second Ace realized what was about to happen. He ducked out of the way but lost his footing. Once Radar's head was clear he looked around. To his horror he spotted Ace dangling below. His belt had caught on a knot in the branch and the bat was swinging helplessly to and fro, his helmet and goggles askew.

Rocket and Swoop caught sight of Ace and burst out laughing, which made Ace even crosser.

"Don't just stand there," he scowled. "Get me out of here."

"Serves him right for all this silly uniform nonsense," Swoop winked at Radar. "He was getting too big for his boots."

At last Ace got to his feet. He put his helmet on straight and harrumphed a few times. Standing well back, he looked questioningly at Radar's scarf.

"Aunt Bathilda knitted it for me," Radar squeaked.

Swoop and Rocket looked at each other – that explained everything. Radar's Aunt Bathilda was well known on the island. Nothing escaped her; she was a formidable character with eyes as sharp as laser beams and a voice that could shatter solid rock. Aunt Bathilda was also convinced that she was a great cook and an expert knitter. Unfortunately, whatever emerged from her cave was rarely digestible or wearable, but it was a very brave bat indeed who told her so.

"She said I should wear it to keep off the flu and if I took it off she would want to know why. I'll put it in my pocket and tell Aunt Bathilda that you said I should."

"Oh, no ... er, carry on," stuttered Ace.

"Your aunt's absolutely right, you can wear it for as long as you like. But what's with all this sneezing business? Whoever heard of a fruit-bat with flu? All we eat is fruit, we're supposed to be healthy. In future keep your sneezes to yourself, you're more dangerous than a ship full of vampirates."

Radar suddenly shivered and it wasn't just because of the flu. It was about a year ago that the fruitbats had encountered the dreaded vampirates and their terrifying leader, Captain Blood. The bloodthirsty buccaneers were planning to attack Fruit Isle and steal the treasure chest hidden in the island's caves. Thanks to the Fruit Gang they had been defeated, and had been last seen sailing their ship, *The Black Fang*, over the horizon.

Radar had been the hero of that wonderful day, but now it all seemed a long, long time ago. He snuffled miserably as he remembered some of his disasters since, like the time they had been playing hide and seek. They were supposed to be finding Swoop, only Radar had got himself lost and had had to be rescued. Then there was the fruit-pip-spitting contest when Radar had been determined to beat Rocket. He had taken a deep, long breath – and choked on his prune stone. Only Aunt Bathilda's timely intervention had saved him.

Radar winced at the memory and glanced nervously over his shoulder. Rocket saw him and laughed. "There's nothing to worry about. We taught those vampirates a lesson. They'll never dare show their ugly mugs around here again."

"Too right they won't," Ace agreed. "Now inspection's over it's time for Operation Flying Practice. We'll play tag. You're 'it', Radar."

"Hey, what…?" Before Radar could react, the others had all peeled away and begun darting through the air. Radar stiffly flew after them. He was beginning to feel worse and there was something he had to tell the others – maybe he could do it at the end of the meeting.

Stars twinkled in the night sky. In the bright moonlight the Fruit Gang darted around near the beach while other fruitbats flitted around their mountain homes on the other side of the island. All seemed perfectly normal and calm, but if the fruitbats hadn't been so busy they might have noticed the strange silence that hung like the shadow of a hangman's noose over a nearby island. If they hadn't been so occupied with their own affairs they might have heard the warning cry of a lone albatross high up in the sky and they might have spotted a wise old turtle swimming away as fast as his flippers would take him. As it was, only Swoop spotted a strange flash of light on the island across the bay but he was too busy swerving out of Rocket's reach to mention it to the others.

* * *

"Put your cutlass away, Mr Leech. Brute force won't work here, we must employ some cunning." A cold voice sliced through the air. At the base of the jagged cliffs, dark shapes suddenly detached themselves from the grey boulders. They had been so still it was almost as though the rocks had come to life. Moonlight picked out details on the shadowy group, glinting off a dagger, a telescope and a pair of bright, white fangs.

"Look at those fools," Captain Blood hissed. "Those fruitbats thought they could beat me. I will teach them to meddle in matters out of their altitude. I want my revenge and I want that treasure."

"That's where they keep all those lovely jewels and glittering gold coins," a fat vampirate said, pointing to the mountain that dominated Fruit Isle. "But there's a whole maze of caves and tunnels in there. The treasure chest will be as hard to find as a vampirate who's afraid of the dark. They may even have got that old battle axe of a fruitbat guarding it. I don't want to tangle with her again, not for all the blood in Transgoldania."

"Thank you, Bo'sun Bones," the captain muttered, drawing a dagger. "But I would advise you to stick to the point in hand or I will stick you with the point in my hand."

The bo'sun kept quiet and the captain's bloodshot eyes roved over Fruit Isle. He couldn't attack the fruitbats, as they would just be able to retreat into the caves and hide with their treasure. Captain Blood picked up a pebble and slowly began crushing it in one hand. Powder was trickling through his fingers when he spotted the Fruit Gang down near the beach.

"Those are the ones who tricked me last time," he hissed, tight-lipped with anger. He followed their games until gradually his expression changed and a look of cunning spread over his face. "Of course, I've cracked it! I have a plan, you scurvy swabs and it's even more fiendishly clever than usual. Everything I need is aboard *The Black Fang*. Let us go back before sun up so I can plot my revenge."

As he said his final words, the captain swirled his cape around him and flew off into the night. The air was filled with the sound of beating wings and a dark spiral, like a cloud of locusts, cast a black shadow over the island.

Just before dawn the Fruit Gang landed back in their tree base. Rocket began demolishing some nearby pears while Ace organized the next meeting.

"We'll rendezvous tomorrow and I expect turn-out to improve noticeably. The pass-word will be raspberries. Any other matters?"

Radar cleared his throat hesitantly. It was now or never. He ought to tell the others. "Ahem." He faltered when he saw the others looking at him, then continued. "I've got some news. My cousin is visiting the island this summer. I've often mentioned the gang and Loopy – that's my cousin's name – really wants to join. Would that be OK?"

"Oh, no," Rocket groaned. "There can't be another Radar. It's dangerous enough with you flying around. If there's two of you it'll be safer to get out of the air."

"Well, that depends," Ace said. "What's this cousin of yours like?"

"Oh, Loopy's a good flyer with a great sense of adventure. Something always seems to happen when Loopy's around. The name comes from loop-the-loops by the way, not because my cousin's mad or anything."

"Well, in that case, I don't see any problems. Bring him along to our next meeting and we'll decide then. OK?"

Radar nodded and took off after the others. Swoop slowed down and flew beside him for a while.

"Are you all right?" he asked. "I wouldn't worry about your cousin, he sounds cool."

Radar smiled weakly but inside his heart was pounding. There was one thing he hadn't mentioned about Loopy, something he didn't dare tell the others. Still, they would find out tomorrow!

Chapter 2

"B… B … BUT, SHE'S A GIRL!" Ace broke the silence in a voice shrill enough to wake up a three-toed sloth and send it scurrying for cover.

"Oh, well done, ten out of ten for observation," Loopy replied. Wing-tips on hips, she casually blew up a bubble gum balloon then BANG she popped it.

If Radar hadn't been feeling so full of flu he might have burst out laughing – the expressions on the other fruitbats' faces were so funny. Ace was goggle-eyed with amazement, even though he wasn't wearing his goggles; Swoop looked as if he had just had a mid-air collision; and Rocket looked as though he was having trouble swallowing – which in fact he was.

Radar had been worrying about the meeting ever since he had been told that Loopy would be coming on a flying visit, and it had made him feel even worse. His nose was all bunged up and now it was beginning to get to his ears – which is bad news if you have ears as big as a fruitbat. However, he had managed to get down from his bed and meet his cousin earlier that evening. Loopy had arrived bang on time, chewing gum and wearing her denim jacket as always.

"Hiya." She squinted at Radar's scarf then offered him some gum. "How's tricks?" After a quick snack with Radar's family she was keen to explore. First stop, the Fruit Gang meeting. They were about to leave when they were reminded that Aunt Bathilda was expecting to see them later that night and there was no arguing with Aunt Bathilda – even by Loopy.

"So what are we waiting for?" said Loopy, taking off. "Let's go. You can show me the way. Once I've joined your gang we can visit Aunt Bathilda. I can't wait to meet the others after what you told me about them."

As they flew towards the Fruit Gang's base, Radar racked his brains. What stories had he told Loopy? He soon found out.

"So you're the ones who needed Radar to help you beat off a hundred vampirates," Loopy said. "And you're the one who ate so much once that he couldn't take off."

Ace and Rocket looked surprised, then glared at Radar. Radar gulped. Maybe he had exaggerated a little. Hurriedly, he tried to change the subject.

"I don't dow about dat," he began. "ATTISCHOO... But what about Loopy joiding the gang?"

"You can't be serious," exclaimed Ace. "Loopy can't be in our gang."

"But why not…?"

"I'd have thought it was obvious. Because she's … you know, well, she's not what we were expecting. She's a … she's a girl."

"So what difference does dat make?" Radar asked.

"Well…" Ace stopped to think for a few moments. "Well, um, because it, er, it's far too dangerous for a girl. And besides, she won't be able to keep up with us, you know the sort of thing…"

"Well I certainly don't know the sort of thing you're talking about," interrupted Loopy. "I'll prove how good I am at flying. I challenge any of you to a race."

Ace rubbed his hands. "OK then, Swoop will accept."

"Dat's not fair," Radar piped up. "Dobody's ever beaten Swoop."

Loopy silenced him with a sign. "I agree,

first to that tree and back. GO!" Before
Swoop could move, Loopy had gone. Radar
smiled as Ace looked startled then shoved
Swoop after her.

"Come on, Loopy, come on," Radar
whispered under his breath. He hardly dared
watch the two bats as they darted through the
night sky. Loopy was quick, already she had
reached the tree and was coming back. She
was ahead of Swoop, but he was catching up
fast. With strong, powerful flaps he began to
haul himself back into contention. Now
Swoop was in Loopy's slipstream. He was
just about to overtake her when suddenly
she flew straight up in the air, looped-the-
loop and ended up on Swoop's tail. What was
going on? Radar watched as she took
something out of her mouth and stuck it to
Swoop's wings. On the next flap he began to
struggle; his wings seemed stuck together.
Loopy glided past and landed effortlessly
beside Ace.

"Satisfied?" She smiled as Swoop flopped down on the branch.

"I don't believe it," Ace gasped in amazement. "How did you do that? Swoop's never even been flown close in a race."

"Just a little trick with bubble gum," Loopy explained. "No hard feelings, I hope."

"It's OK," grinned Swoop. "You beat me. Welcome to the gang."

"Hold on a second," interrupted Ace. "Loopy may have beaten you but she still can't join the gang. For a start, she doesn't have an ID card and she doesn't know our passwords. She's chewing gum, not wearing regulation clothing, and..."

"If those are the most important things to you then I don't want to be in your crummy gang," Loopy smiled sweetly. "I thought the Fruit Gang might have adventures and explore new places but I was obviously wrong. Come on, Radar, this is boring. We've got more interesting things to do – like visiting Aunt Bathilda."

Ace fixed Radar with an angry stare. "If you leave, Radar, you'll be leaving the Fruit Gang too."

Radar hung rooted to the branch in between Ace and Loopy. This wasn't fair. What should he do? He didn't know which way to go. Why did things like this always seem to happen to him? If he went with Loopy, he'd be out of the gang but if he didn't go then he'd have to face Aunt Bathilda. That settled it! Radar shrugged his shoulders to apologize then followed his cousin. The remaining fruitbats watched as the duo flew over the mountain and disappeared from sight. Swoop was the first to break the silence.

"That wasn't a cool thing to do, Ace. The gang won't be the same without Radar and that was a clever trick Loopy played on me. It would be fun if she joined and let's face it, we could do with some fun. We haven't done anything exciting for ages. Loopy was right, it is boring."

"Just hold on, wait a minute," Ace began. "Of course we can have a good time without those two … let's, um…" Ace's brain raced. Maybe he had been wrong, but he didn't want to be shown up in front of the others. His eyes darted around the island. This was crunch time, he had to come up with something good. He could see that Swoop and Rocket were not bluffing. They were getting ready to fly home. What could he do?

Out of the corner of his eye he caught sight of something – there, gently rocking in the surf at the edge of the beach. It was some wreckage, the remains of a rowing boat. This could be the stroke of luck he wanted.

"I know what to do," he yelled. "We'll explore the wreckage on the beach."

A few seconds later Ace was darting around the wreck. He glided over the gunwhale then started waving frantically at the others. Swoop sighed but he and Rocket took off and hovered above Ace. A horrible smell wafted up from the green seaweed that was snagged on the splintered planks. There was something odd about the battered boat. Maybe it was the blackened timbers or the sound of the tiller creaking as if it was being steered by an invisible ghostly helmsman. Swoop felt the hair on the back of his neck stand up on end. Pull yourself together, he thought. Luckily Ace distracted him by reaching into the boat and pulling out a bottle.

"So, it's a bottle. Big deal."

"No, it's more than that – look, there's a message inside it."

Swoop and Rocket saw a thick piece of parchment rolled up inside the green glass. They flew closer while Ace gently pulled out a yellow, salt-water stained document.

"Oww!" A thin line of red slowly appeared on Ace's finger. "I've cut myself on the paper."

Swoop shivered and looked over his shoulder. What was wrong with him? He didn't normally get the jitters like this. It was probably the excitement. Rocket tried to snatch the paper from Ace, saying, "It's only a little cut, hurry up, what does it say?"

Drops of blood dripped from Ace's finger on to the parchment, staining it with vivid red spots, but Ace didn't seem to notice. His eyes opened wide as he began to read. This was incredible. What an amazing stroke of luck. The others would soon forget about Radar and Loopy when they saw what the message said. This was better than his wildest dreams. Already he began planning the expedition tomorrow night. Ace looked triumphantly at Swoop and Rocket.

"I think that when you hear this you'll realize that the Fruit Gang is the most exciting thing going and that we don't need Radar or his cousin to have adventures. I will let you in on it as long as you agree that I'm the best leader of the Fruit Gang."

"OK, OK," Rocket sighed impatiently. "Get on with it, what does the message say?"

Ace smiled and cleared his throat. He began to read:

> *From Captain C. Salt. Here is my sad tale. In the year 1885 my galleon, the good ship* Revenge, *foundered on the reef surrounding Shipwreck Island. I am the only survivor, all my crew perished, only the* Revenge's *cargo survived.*
>
> *We were carrying treasure worth a king's ransom. This was washed ashore in a large chest. I took the treasure chest and hid it at the end of my cave that overlooks Shark Straits.*
>
> *Here I keep watch for passing ships but food and water are running low. I fear there is little hope of rescue... My strength fading fast... I only hope someone learns of my fate...*

It took a few seconds to sink in. Rocket's eyes opened wide in disbelief. He snatched the note and reread it. WOW! They were going on a treasure hunt. He took off and flew excitedly around the beach.

"See what I mean?" Ace asked, smirking. "We shall need shovels. You two can carry them while I'm in charge of finding the treasure chest. Meet here tomorrow at nightfall and don't tell anyone about this. This is an operation for Fruit Gang members only and no one else. This'll teach Radar and Loopy. Boring indeed!"

Ace chuckled as he took off. He flew home with Rocket, leaving Swoop on the beach feeling uneasy. It was not fair to exclude Radar. It would be terrible to miss out on their biggest adventure since defeating the vampirates. Radar had been vital then and if he missed out on the treasure hunt, he would probably never be in the gang again.

Swoop scratched his head. At last he made up his mind. "I'll tell Radar about it all tomorrow night," he muttered. "He can decide if he wants to come and if he brings Loopy, all the better."

Chapter 3

Radar was struggling to keep up with Loopy, who was flapping furiously ahead.

"What a welcome that was," she muttered angrily under her breath. "Your friend Ace has got all the good manners of a charging rhino."

"I'b sure he didn't bean id," snuffled Radar. "Dhey're nice really, dhey just need a bit of time to get used to you."

"Well I'm not going to wait for them," pronounced Loopy. "They'll just have to manage without us. I know that I can manage without all those rules ... *she doesn't have an ID card, doesn't know passwords, chews gum blah, blah, blah...*"

Radar looked in surprise at his cousin. Her impression of Ace was spot on, she sounded just like him. It hadn't calmed her down, though.

"Where's this cave, anyway?" she asked.

"If you'd just slow down a liddle, I'll show you." Radar took the lead. He flew past the main caves, down a narrow ravine and stopped. He pointed away and up to his right. Just visible behind a thick bush was a gap in the rocks – the entrance to Aunt Bathilda's cave.

"Oh, do, what's dat?' grimaced Radar as they flew closer. Despite the flu, his nostrils were being attacked by a terrible smell, worse even than school dinners, that was wafting towards them. The awful realization suddenly hit Radar like a broadside from the vampirates' cannons: this could only mean one thing – it was Aunt Bathilda's cooking night!

The fruitbats took a deep breath and glided gently into the cave. Loopy looked around in amazement. Aunt Bathilda's home was absolutely crammed full of the most amazing things. The walls were covered with pictures and photos while strange furniture and unusual objects took up the entire floor. Loopy stared at the uniflycycle and some juggling clubs.

"Aunt B doesn't believe in cave work," Radar muttered. "She says she's always too busy with other things – like poisoning innocent relatives or knitting them horrible clothes!"

"Well, I think Aunt Bathilda is great," Loopy replied. "But where is she?"

Just then a large cloud of black smoke billowed out towards the duo. Once they had finished coughing they saw Aunt Bathilda. She was closing the oven door and was wearing an apron. Her eyebrows were singed and her cheeks were black with soot. She was carrying a large steaming bowl – Radar didn't dare look to see what was inside it.

"Hello, you two," she smiled. "It's good to see you again, Loopy. Welcome to my humble abode."

"It's amazing," Loopy gasped. "I've never seen anywhere like it."

"I'm so glad you like it. Would you like the twopenny tour?" Before Loopy could reply, Bathilda had started. "I'll just leave this here to cool," she said, putting the bowl down on a table in the far corner of the room. To his horror, Radar noticed that the table's surface was covered with other bowls and dishes.

"Be careful of Sidney," Aunt Bathilda warned as they flitted through the cave. "He's harmless really, it's just that snakes don't like being landed on."

Radar noticed with some satisfaction that even Loopy was slightly surprised by that, but soon his cousin's attention was attracted by something else. She was mesmerized by a huge pair of antlers mounted on a wall. "Oh, yes, the giant stag beetle – nasty fellow. He attacked me when I was on an expedition to visit some friends up the Orinoco. I've still got the boat I sailed in. It's loaded to the gunwhales and moored at the back entrance to the cave, just in case I feel the adventuring urge again… Oh, but look here – these are the ancestors."

A series of dark-framed pictures and sepia-toned photos were hanging on the wall that led up to Bathilda's favourite sleeping stalactite. Radar and Loopy hovered in mid-air as Bathilda pointed to the first picture. "There's the great, great, great grandaddy of them all, Battilla. He was supposed to be very stern, a bit of a bully even."

"Reminds me of someone," Radar muttered. "I wonder who?"

"Now then, Radar, pay attention! Ah, here is Great, Great Uncle Battersby; then there is Great Auntie Flutter, who was rumoured to be a bit flighty. She went into the military side of the family when she married Major Blunder's batman … then beside them is my second cousin Swift, who played winger for the Fruit Flyers."

Aunt Bathilda's wing brushed the top of the next photograph, showering Radar with dust, some surprised woodworm and a bit of mouldy cheese. He sneezed loudly.

"Bless you, Radar. Still, flu or not, you must keep up. Now this is one of my favourites, your great uncle Baticcelli. He was very clever, a great painter and a batchelor of arts. He painted all these pictures on the wall."

"What happened to him?"

Bathilda tapped her forehead. "He got a bit … well, you know, bats in the belfry."

"Oh, that's sad."

"Yes, it was. It got so bad he ended up head-master of the local school."

"That explains a lot of things," Radar muttered.

"Then we move on to Radar's side of the family. This is his uncle Crumple. He was a smashing chap who tried to make it in films as a stunt bat. People said he was ideally qualified for the job, but unfortunately one of his sky dives turned into a nose dive. Needless to say his career never really took off after that... Then, last of all, there's Batrick Moore the astronomer, and poor old Professor Barnstormer. She met with a terrible accident in her laboratory, tragic really, just when she thought she'd perfected her automatic desiccating machine..."

"What a brilliant family, thank you for showing us the pictures."

"You're welcome, my dear. I'm just glad some young people are still interested in them," Aunt Bathilda replied, staring sternly over her half-moon glasses at Radar. "I've got lots of family relics, or 'airlooms' as I like to call them, scattered about. You're welcome to have a look through them if you wish, though please give me a shout if you find Sidney."

"I'm sure we will," gulped Radar. He wasn't very interested in the relics, but he was happy to hover behind Loopy if it kept him out of his aunt's reach. Unfortunately, Bathilda had other ideas.

"Before you do that I'm sure you must be hungry. You're in luck, I've been cooking. You can be the first to try my new recipes – I've been experimenting."

Radar gulped – he'd rather taste some of the experiments that came out of Dr Frankenstein's laboratory than Aunt Bathilda's creations – but his aunt spotted him trying to sneak out of the cave and fixed her gaze full on him.

"And I've been busy making something extra special to help you shake off that flu, young man. With a mystery ingredient."

Radar squeaked – the last mystery ingredient had turned out to be a red hot chilli pepper which was so hot that he'd had to gulp water for two days before he could cool down. What would it be this time?

"This is my latest attempt and I'm sure I've got it right this time." Radar went white when he saw what Aunt Bathilda was trying to hack up into slices. It was a Battenberg cake. This really was kill or cure time. Aunt Bathilda had had so many efforts at baking this cake and trying it out on unwary bats that it was nick-named BATTEN-down-the-hatches-your-tastebuds-are-about-to-collide-with-an-ice-BERG CAKE. The mere mention of it had the most miraculous effect on bats all over the island. Young bats would leap out of their sickbeds to sit exams at school while old fruit-bats suddenly discovered a new lease of life and flew faster than they thought possible. It was also rumoured to be typhoon-proof and very effective at warding off tidal waves.

"No, no, really, we ought to be going," Radar stammered. He flew backwards into a corner as Aunt Bathilda advanced on him, a slab of cake balanced on a fork. Radar felt solid rock behind him – he could retreat no further. He braced himself; there was no way he was going to eat it.

"Mmm … mmm," the killer cake was getting closer. Radar touched the rock face behind him – and it moved. It made a hissing noise and slithered out of his grasp. Radar suddenly realized where Sidney had got to! He opened his mouth to scream, and Aunt Bathilda saw her chance and moved like lightning. Before Radar knew what he had done, he had swallowed.

"There, that wasn't so bad now, was it?" she asked.

Radar stood still, not daring to move. He could feel the cake plummeting down into his stomach, where it stopped for a few seconds – like a ticking time bomb. Then it exploded! The topping whizzed around his windpipe like a whirling waltzer, fragments of sponge began playing bumper cars inside his stomach and a strange, bitter taste went on a roller-coaster, white-knuckle ride through his veins.

"W ... what's in it?" he gasped through the tears.

"Garlic," replied Aunt Bathilda, helping him to his feet. "It's good for the blood, you know. I read that it adds a certain something extra. I've been growing it on a nearby island, I was planning to add it to all my cakes."

"It's a good idea," Loopy said, staring at Radar. "But I'm not sure your public's ready for it yet."

Loopy broke off as Radar had a coughing fit. She managed to stand him up, then he hiccuped. A few seconds later he coughed again. "Hic, cough, hic, cough." Radar bounced across the cave, unable to speak.

"It's never had that effect before," Aunt Bathilda muttered, looking concernedly at Radar. "Maybe I did overdo the garlic a tiny little bit. I wonder what will cure hiccups?"

"Water?" suggested Loopy. Aunt Bathilda

smiled and filled a glass. Radar took a slurp. He hiccupped the water down then coughed it out, spraying Loopy.

Aunt Bathilda looked thoughtful. "Hmmm. I think we might need some stronger medicine. Now where is that thing?"

While Aunt Bathilda rooted through the heirlooms, Radar tried to hiccup quietly out of the cave but there was no way out. His escape route was barred by his aunt.

"This is one of Professor Barnstorm's inventions – her patented anti-hiccupping device." In her right hand was a small box covered in rich red velvet with a gold clasp. It looked as though it should contain jewellery.

"Now, Radar, get a good, close look at the box … that's it. And now I will release the catch."

BOING! CRASH. Radar leapt into the air as a huge, hairy spider sprang out of the box at him.

"See, it's a Jack-in-the-Box," Aunt Bathilda

explained once Radar had been lifted from the floor and was propped up against his cousin. "It's supposed to surprise you so you stop hiccupping. Has it worked?"

Radar was unable to utter a word. "I take it that that's a yes, then," smiled his aunt. "There's no need to thank me, I'm just pleased it's all cleared up." She gave the box to Loopy. "You should keep this in case of another attack. I will see you tomorrow. It's knitting night, we'll see what I can rustle up for you."

Loopy smiled and flew Radar out of the cave. He flinched when he saw the box in her hand. Loopy handed it over to him. "Well, Aunt Bathilda is remarkable. I can see this holiday is going to turn out to be a lot of fun. How are you feeling? Has the cake done the trick?"

Radar made the only reply he could. He turned miserably to his cousin and went, "ATTISCHOOOOOOOO!"

Chapter 4

After visiting Aunt Bathilda, Radar slept very badly. Strange dreams flashed through his head throughout the day. He was imagining himself as a fire-breathing dragon whose breath scorched trees and could strip paint off walls from a hundred paces when he was woken by someone shaking his shoulder.

"W ... what's going on?" he breathed. Radar heard a thud. He cleared the sleep from his eyes and saw Swoop staggering to his feet. "Hello, Swoop, what are you doing here? Are you OK?"

Swoop held his hand up to his face and tried not to breathe in.

"What have you been eating?" he gasped. "Hold it, that's close enough."

Radar struggled to focus. His stomach was about as calm as a pool of bubbling lava and his ears felt as if they were full of cotton wool. He could see Swoop's lips moving but he couldn't make out what he was saying. Only a faint voice, as if from far away, carried through into his head. Radar cocked his ears and tried to lip-read.

"We've found this amazing boat – with a treasure map…"

What on earth did Swoop mean – *they'd found a blazing float with a leisure nap?*

"Ace doesn't want you and Loopy to come, but it would be great if you could join us on Shipwreck Island. I'm sure you know it. We'll be going to wrecker's rock before gliding on to the island surrounded by a reef."

They'll be going to catch a cough before hiding

on the island surrounded by beef. Radar stared at Swoop in disbelief. He looked fine but what was he gibbering about? Maybe Aunt Bathilda had tried out a particularly exotic recipe on him.

"I'll see you then, by the shark straits at ten. And bring Loopy."

I'll see you then by the sharp gates at ten, and ring Droopy? Before Radar could stop him, Swoop was gone. Radar looked around at the cave and pinched himself. Was he still asleep? Had he just been dreaming? He shook his head to try and unscramble his wits then he decided to tell Loopy – she might be able to make sense of it all.

Radar got down from the ceiling and glided across to the guest cave. He blew his nose loudly to announce his presence. Loopy smiled at him over her banana breakfast. As Radar flew closer the smile melted on Loopy's face and her nose wrinkled up.

"Phew, what a whiff! Aunt Bathilda must

have gone into garlic overload. Have some of this, it's peppermint flavour."

Radar took the bubble gum that Loopy offered and began chewing. POP. The fuzzy feeling in his head started to clear. He could think straight and hear properly again. Radar told Loopy about Swoop's visit. She frowned.

"Hmmm. It sounds like a wind-up to me. I think they're trying to pull our legs. I mean, what was Swoop talking about?"

"Maybe I couldn't hear Swoop properly because of my flu. He looked excited, I'm sure he was trying to tell me something important. Hold on, I think I've got it. Swoop mentioned this meeting at ten o'clock, but I've never heard of somewhere with sharp gates. Unless … there is one island with a sharp coral reef that's a bit like a gate for ships. When the tide is low, the reef shuts off the island but when the tide is high you can sail over the coral spikes."

"I suppose that could be it. I guess we can

check it out. If this is Ace's idea of a joke, though, or some sort of ambush, he'll be sorry."

A few seconds later they were outside the cave. Loopy's nose twitched with curiosity. "Look at that," she whispered.

Radar stared up at the sky. The moon glared down at him like a bloodshot eye. The whole of Fruit Isle was withering under its angry red stare; the trees and mountain looked as if they were on fire with black shadows flickering between the flaming colour. The sea was calm, dead calm. No flying fish jumped playfully out of the water and no birds circled overhead. An air of brooding silence hung heavily over the island.

"I have got a strange feeling that something is about to happen," whispered Loopy. "This is going to be a night to remember, I can feel it in my wings."

Radar and Loopy took off and headed south towards their destination. Trailing in his cousin's slipstream, Radar looked down at the clear water below. Although the surface was perfectly still, a few fathoms down, the ocean was alive with swirling and thrashing. Colours dived and swam before Radar's eyes as fishes darted through weeds then disappeared into coral caves. Radar had never seen anything like it. What did it mean? He wanted to tell Loopy but by the time he caught up with her the ocean was calm again. It seemed that everyone was behaving strangely tonight.

"There it is," announced Radar.

"I can't imagine there's much to do here," Loopy said, staring at the flat, marshy island ahead. "I suggest we stick together and look for the others. It shouldn't take long. Keep your eyes peeled just in case your friends have got some trick lined up for us."

The duo flew low over the centre of the island, hugging the contours of the ground. A few tufts of grass dotted the marshy coastline while inland a cluster of small trees struggled to grow some shrivelled oranges. I doubt this is Rocket's favourite feeding ground, thought Radar.

"There's no sign of them here," Loopy said. "Where could they be?"

Radar spotted a cave. "I'll check it out," he said, trying to sound braver than he felt. He flew towards the rocky entrance. Looking into the gloom ahead he saw a long, thin tunnel. The roof had collapsed further along and large cracks ran in jagged lines along the roof.

"Me and my big mouth," Radar gulped, venturing inside. "Hello, Swoop. Are you there?" The only response was the sound of stones clattering further ahead. Was that them? "Come on, Ace. Come out now, Rocket … ocket … ket." The walls of the cave threw Radar's voice back at him. Where were the others? Either he had got the message wrong or even Swoop was playing games with him. Radar shrugged his shoulders and turned around.

As he flew out of the cave his right wing-tip clipped a clump of strange plants. They fell over, releasing a familiar smell. Radar looked at the roots. There, half-covered with soil, were garlic cloves. He had stumbled over Aunt Bathilda's herb garden. Radar stuffed the garlic in his pocket, intending to give it to his aunt when he saw her – just as long as he wasn't invited round for tea.

"What kept you?" Loopy enquired. She pointed at the sky. Huge, threatening black clouds were obscuring the horizon and a stiff breeze was starting to blow.

"I think it's time to go," she said. Radar agreed. As they left the small island, the wind picked up. Below their wings, the sea's flat surface began to ripple. Waves threw white spray up into the air. The fruitbats flew higher as the wind grew stronger.

"That was not my idea of a joke." Loopy had to shout to make herself heard. "Swoop's sent us off on a wild goose chase. I bet the

Fruit Gang are back in their caves chuckling." There was a glint of anger in her eye that brooked no argument. Radar kept his head down and concentrated on flying against the wind. At last they saw Fruit Isle. Radar was looking forward to hanging around to recover, but there was to be no rest that night.

They flew into the cave — and almost collided with Aunt Bathilda! Once Radar had recovered from the shock he looked around and saw that the cave was full! All his family were there asking questions and shouting at the tops of their voices.

What was going on? After Radar and Loopy explained where they had been, Aunt Bathilda stepped in. "I think it's just as well you didn't find the Fruit Gang," she said. "We know where they are."

Radar and Loopy looked at each other as Aunt Bathilda handed them a flying helmet. Radar recognized it instantly as Ace's. Inside it was a message.

The two fruitbats took the piece of paper and read the spidery writing.

I have taken some unusual booty on board — three of your bratty bats. If you ever want to see them again, load the treasure chest on to your ship and sail to Port o' Plunder on my island, Transgoldania. Do not try any tricks or Castle Blood will be their final mooring place. Rest assured, they are well guarded. I have sworn by the hilt of a seadog's cutlass that not even Hurricane Harry will help them to escape. I will expect you at midnight two nights from now.

"Maybe it's another joke," Loopy scowled. "How do we know this is genuine?"

"Just look at the signature," answered Aunt Bathilda.

Loopy moved her thumb. Radar peered over her shoulder and what he saw made the blood freeze in his veins. The message was signed by someone he had hoped he would never see or hear from again: Captain Blood

The full realization of what had happened struck Radar like one of Rocket's playful punches. He staggered back towards the cave entrance. Just then a loud crash shook the whole island and lightning forked down through the sky. The flash of bright light illuminated a familiar shape on the horizon. Radar caught a fleeting glimpse of a tall, dark ship. With all sails billowing and the Jolly Roger flapping, *The Black Fang* was sailing for home. And somewhere aboard her were Ace, Rocket and Swoop!

Chapter 5

Crash! A noise like thunder and a flash of white light woke Ace. His head was aching, his breakfast was pitching and heaving in his stomach – what was going on? His thoughts were as tangled as his arms and legs. Ace tried to move but a great weight was lying across him. Something was blocking his mouth too. He spat out something that looked like a wing – it *was* a wing! Ace traced it along an arm, back to a shoulder, a neck and then up to a familiar face.

"Get off, will you, Rocket," Ace grunted,

pushing the large fruitbat away. As some breathing space appeared, cold water slapped him in the face. He looked down and saw rough sea below. The wind was blowing white spray off the crest of waves. Ace shook away the salt water then craned his neck for a better look upwards. He spotted a pair of feet sticking out under Rocket's left wing – they were Swoop's. The trio were in a net that was hanging from the bowsprit of a ship. In the rough weather they were swinging to and fro like a clock's pendulum.

"I feel terrible," groaned Rocket. "I think I'm going to die."

"We can't be having that," a voice answered cheerfully. "Not yet, anyway. Our catch is waking up. Haul 'em in, shipmates."

The net suddenly dipped forwards then swung around the bows of the ship. Ace looked over Rocket's shoulder and gasped. The bony fingers of the ship's figurehead scraped past him and for a second he found himself teeth to teeth with a grinning skeleton before BANG, hitting the wooden deck.

"Ouch! What's going on? Where are we?" The landing jolted Swoop into consciousness. Instinctively, he tried to stand up. The ship lurched sideways in the heavy swell and Swoop groggily fell over Rocket. Hearty guffaws rang around the ship. "Don't worry you land-lubbers, you'll soon get your sea-wings. I love this weather."

At that moment lightning streaked from the sky, illuminating a terrifying scene. The wind was howling all around, tearing at the ship's sails and whipping up the sea into a boiling, seething rage. Waves were hurling themselves at the ship. High above the fruitbats' heads the skull and crossbones of the Jolly Roger swayed and rippled as if it was performing a macabre dance. In front of the trio loomed a familiar face. Fangs glistening and skull tattoos glinting under each wing, Captain Blood had the fruitbats right where he wanted them.

"I can't tell you how delighted I am to see you again," the vampirate hissed. "My entire crew's been waiting for this moment. Your old friends have been missing you."

The fruitbats looked across the main deck of *The Black Fang*. The whole bloodthirsty crew of bite-throats were watching them. The sight of two vampirates in particular made the fruitbats gulp – Mr Leech, the tall, thin mate of the ship, and Bo'sun Bones, his barrel-shaped sidekick.

Mr Leech flew across the deck. He yawned, showing off a pair of fangs that were green and smelt of stale seaweed.

"I imagine you're hungry," he said to Rocket. "Luckily, I have some biscuits here." The fruitbats watched as Mr Leech bit open a packet. He dangled them in front of Rocket, then snatched them away. "There's just one little thing missing from these," he said, examining them. "Ship's biscuits are famous for one thing – weevils! Unfortunately these

53

don't seem to have any. Let's see if we can remedy that."

The vampirate took a tooth-pick from his pocket and scraped it under his long finger-nails.

"Ah, ha," he exclaimed. "Success." Mr Leech pulled out the toothpick – hanging from the sharp piece of wood were three wriggling weevils. He transferred the worms from the toothpick on to a biscuit. The weevils immediately began burrowing into the doughy surface. "That's much better," grinned Mr Leech. "Any takers?"

The fruitbats backed away from the grub-filled offering until BUMP, they hit a solid object – it was Bo'sun Bones. Diamonds glittered in his eye-patch and moonlight reflected off a gold tooth. He was juggling with some familiar objects. The fruitbats recognized a catapult, a badge, a penknife, a sandwich box and a pair of sunglasses. They checked their pockets – they were all empty.

"You can't treat us like this," Ace said, standing as tall as he could. He rearranged his scarf, polished his goggles and went to put his helmet straight. "What this? Where's my helmet?"

Captain Blood replied, "I'm afraid I used it to send a message to your friends. It was handy as proof of your capture. Useful things, messages. Do you remember this one?" The vampirate motioned to Bo'sun Bones who produced a green bottle with a familiar scrap of parchment in it. "Rather well written in my opinion. Oh, you should have seen your faces when you began to read that bit about the buried treasure. Laugh? I could have died – except, of course, I can't. I knew you couldn't resist and I was right. It was wonderful to watch you flying to Shipwreck Island for your treasure hunt. Only it wasn't treasure you found, was it?"

Ace stared back defiantly although his heart was sinking inside. They had swallowed the vampirate's bait hook, line and sinker. He remembered leading the others to Shipwreck Island. They were flying slowly because they were loaded down with shovels and pickaxes. There was no wind and everything was still, as if the trees were holding their breath, waiting for something to happen. Ace had led Swoop and Rocket into the cave overlooking Shark Straits. At the far end was a treasure chest, just like the message said.

Now he knew that it had all been too easy, but then they had gathered around the wooden box. With visions of gleaming gold and glittering jewels lighting up their minds, they struggled to lever open the lid. At last it sprang open to reveal … nothing. As they stared into the empty chest, Captain Blood appeared in front of them as if from out of thin air. Then before they could recover from the shock, their roofs caved in. Ace remembered something dropping heavily on to him, a thud, a flash of light and then he woke up on *The Black Fang*.

"You can do what you want to us," Ace said bravely, ignoring the groan from Rocket. "You'll get no treasure."

"I don't agree," purred Captain Blood. He took a deep breath. "I have never had any sense of smell. Flowers, food or perfume are nothing to me, but today something is in the air – the sweet smell of success. You are not simply my prisoners, you are my hostages. I have sent a ransom note to Fruit Isle. My demands are simple – I will exchange the treasure for you."

"They'll never do it," continued Ace defiantly. "They'll never trust you to…"

The fruitbat broke off as Captain Blood pulled out his cutlass and thrust the tip under Ace's nose. Ace shivered as the cold metal touched his flesh and he looked straight into the vampirate's bloodshot eyes.

"That's enough talking, you'll have plenty of time for that during the voyage. We shall be docking in two nights' time."

The vampirate span round to face his crew. "Set the course, Bo'sun. We're sailing home. Stow 'em in the hold."

Instantly the ship's deck and rigging swarmed with vampirates. Ace caught a last glimpse of Fruit Isle before the trio disappeared below decks.

Rocket broke the silence. "This is another fine mess you've got us into. Some treasure hunt this turned out to be. I haven't even got any food left."

"Oh, can't you keep quiet about food for just a few minutes," replied Ace. "I need some peace so I can plan a way out of here."

The fruitbats sank into gloomy silence, each of them alone with their thoughts. While Rocket dreamt hungrily of fruit-laden orchards and Ace racked his brains to find an escape route, Swoop tried to figure out why Radar and Loopy had never appeared on Shipwreck Island. Still, it was just as well they hadn't! He wondered where they were now.

Chapter 6

"So what are we going to do?" Loopy's question hung in the air unanswered.

Radar's heart was pounding as heavily as the rain outside the cave. He felt terrible, he was shivering and giddy with flu.

"What can we do?" he snuffled after a long pause. "You heard what the Flight Leaders said."

Loopy snorted. Earlier that evening, all the fruitbats had met in the assembly cave to debate what course of action they should take. The two eldest and most senior Flight Leaders, Albat and Engelbat, announced the decision.

The fruitbats had no choice but to give in. They would load their treasure chest aboard *The Golden Apple* and, with a hand-picked crew, set sail for Port o' Plunder. Radar and Loopy had been expressly forbidden from embarking with them and had been grounded until *The Golden Apple* returned. Loopy had been reminded that her history project was overdue and Aunt Bathilda had handed Radar his domestic science folder.

"Well, I'm not going to miss all the action," Loopy said. "What are you waiting for? Let's get going."

"B ... but you heard what was said. We've been told to stay on Fruit Isle."

"Surely you're not going to listen to those fuddy-duddies. They're just a bunch of spoil-sports."

"But what about the flu, I feel terrible."

"That'll soon clear up. Come on."

"But how are we going to get there? It's too far to fly – we'll need a boat."

"Don't worry about that. I know where we can get one. Anyway, why all this 'but, but, but' business? You've already met Captain Blood and tricked him. You know what to expect."

Radar gulped. Loopy had put her finger on what was really worrying him. He had beaten Captain Blood once, but that was a long time ago. Since then lots of things had gone wrong for Radar and in the meantime the vampirate would have learnt his lesson. The only thing Radar expected was that it would be a lot harder to outsmart him this time. Also, Radar had been flying with the Fruit Gang then – now it was just him and Loopy – and things had hardly gone wonderfully well since she had arrived on Fruit Isle.

Loopy put her wings on her hips and chewed her gum furiously.

"I must say I expected a bit more enthusiasm," she muttered. "They are your friends, after all."

"So why are you so keen on going?" asked Radar. "What's wrong with leaving it up to the others?"

"I want to watch the action and see these vampirates in the flesh," Loopy replied. "But if something does go wrong I think we should be there. It would be wonderful to show Ace up. I can't wait to see his face if we have to rescue him."

"I think I can wait," Radar muttered.

"Hurry up," hissed Loopy. "We'll just be watching the exchange, I promise. Come on, you've got to come."

Of course Loopy was right. After all, Radar told himself, all they had to do was anchor out of sight and watch the Fruit Gang being handed over for the treasure. Everything would go according to plan and they would be back before anyone noticed they were missing. It wasn't as if he would have to carry out one of Loopy's hair-brained rescue schemes or face up to Captain Blood again.

By the time he had managed to convince himself, his cousin was already out of the cave. Radar tied his scarf tightly round his neck and took off after her. Within seconds he was soaking wet and buffeted by the wind, but he gritted his teeth and caught up. The duo kept low, skimming over – or in Radar's case through – fruit trees. Despite the wind and the rain Radar could hear Aunt Bathilda organizing the loading of *The Golden Apple* well before they could see the ship. They slowed down to a glide to watch as the treasure chest was hoisted aboard.

"We can't let the vampirates get away with this," muttered Radar. "But where are we going?" He soon found out as Loopy landed in a familiar cave – Aunt Bathilda's. What were they doing there?

"We're going to 'borrow' Bathilda's boat." Loopy saw the look on Radar's face. "Don't worry," she added. "Aunt B is sailing with the others, we'll be back before she ever knows."

Radar sighed. The whole expedition was going from dangerous to downright disastrous – like most of his cousin's plans. Now if anything went wrong, they could end up facing both the vampirates and his aunt. Radar's health rating dropped another point but he carried on. He flew through the cave, down a long tunnel and emerged near a quiet inlet. A strange-looking boat was moored nearby.

"Oh, it's a batamaran," said Loopy. "I know how to sail them. Help me cast off."

"Aye, aye, cap'n," Radar muttered under his breath as he untied the mooring ropes. While he untangled himself from the rope Loopy took the helm. Slowly they moved away from the sheltered island waters. The wind filled the sail and the boat began lurching in the choppy seas.

"I … I think I'd better go below," Radar gulped.

"OK," grinned Loopy. "Check on supplies

while you're there, although I've brought a bumper pack of bubble gum just in case."

The last thing Radar wanted to do was look for food, especially if it had been cooked by Aunt Bathilda, but he did as Loopy suggested. The cramped space below decks was packed as full as Aunt Bathilda's cave. Remembering the encounter with Sidney the snake, Radar carefully picked his way through the cabin. He found a drawer full of maps and shouted the news to Loopy. A brief glance in the food cupboard was enough to make Radar want to turn back, but it was too late – Fruit Isle was already out of sight.

Just then Radar heard his name being called. He staggered up on to deck. The roaring wind almost blew him overboard. Grabbing hold of the handrail he looked around. On all sides huge waves were towering up and reaching the sky. Urged on by the howling gale they raced forwards, eager to crash down into the tiny craft. Loopy had tied herself to the rudder where she bellowed instructions to Radar. He wiped salty sea spray from his eyes and hauled down the sails. He joined his cousin in the stern. The two fruitbats hung on grimly and desperately steered the ship into the waves. If they were hit broadsides on they would be sunk without trace. Slowly, slowly the bows turned to face each wave. One minute the sea sucked them down, the next it spat them out. With a bone-jarring crunch they hit the water. There was scarcely time to recover before turning their craft round into the next wave.

All night long the duo battled against the hurricane. Radar counted each wave as it passed. He lost track after thirty then started again. After the eighty-third wave, the fruit-bats noticed a change. Almost unnoticed, dawn was creeping up on them. The sky changed slowly from black to grey to green and on until it was streaked with pink and yellow. The wind began to die down. The sea became calmer. The hurricane's fury had subsided to a mere storm. Loopy gulped down some water.

"I'll take first watch now the worst has passed," she said, hoarsely. "Try and get some sleep, you'll need it for the vampirates."

Radar needed no more prompting. He went below, tucked his head under his wing and was instantly asleep.

While Radar slept, so did the fruitbats aboard *The Black Fang*. Sleep had also been impossible for them during the night as they had banged and rolled around in the blackness of the hull. They were so cold, battered and bruised that when the hurricane blew out, they fell into a deep slumber, too tired and stiff to even think about escaping. Night had fallen again by the time they were woken up by a familiar voice.

"Wake up you lazy lubbers, the captain wants you topside."

With that they were hauled up and dumped on the deck.

"Oww," winced Rocket.

"Belay the noise. You're loud enough to wake the dead, let alone the crew."

"Ignore him," Ace muttered, looking around. The crew didn't look like they needed any waking up. They were packed on deck, drinking grog and grinning at each other. On the poop deck he spotted a group of vampirates holding a strange collection of instruments. One had a pair of cymbals, another a trumpet, one a drum, and there was even a triangle. Bo'sun Bones was holding a wooden leg as if it was a conductor's baton. Ace didn't like the look of things at all.

"Get them out of the net and let them stand up." Captain Blood's orders were obeyed instantly. "My crew need some amusement after our long voyage and I am only too happy to oblige. By the clicking of my fangs, it's time some trickery began."

"What does he mean?" Rocket asked.

"You'll soon find out. Look at me," Captain Blood ordered. "Not the one in the ridiculous flying clothes, I want him to join the spectators. You two, look at me." Something in his voice made Swoop and Rocket stare at the vampirate. "Look into my eyes ... deeply into them ... deeply ... that's right. Now relax ... good ... keep looking ... that's it."

Too late Ace realized what was happening. The two fruitbats were being hypnotized. Ace tried waving his hand in front of their faces but there was not a flicker, not a sign of recognition.

Captain Blood laughed. "Mr Leech, please restrain our prisoner while he watches his two friends. Now let the show begin."

Ace struggled in vain against Leech's bony grip. He watched as the captain beckoned Swoop and Rocket nearer. They walked forwards and listened intently.

"Now you are under my control and will obey my every command. Agreed?"

"Yes," came the response.

"Now, first the large one. You are no longer a heavyweight, you have become a graceful ballet dancer. You will soar and swoop with streamlined skill and elegance. You will start dancing as soon as the beautiful music begins."

Blood gave a signal to his bo'sun. He began waving his wooden leg and the vampirate band struck up. Ace's first reaction was to cover his ears as the awful noise bombarded him. Then, slowly, his mouth opened in amazement, his eyes opened wide and his wings dropped down to his side. Rocket had taken off and was hovering in the air. A huge smile lit up his face and he was fluttering to and fro, round the band, as if they were playing the most melodic music.

After a few seconds, Rocket swept over the band and began attempting pirouettes. The crew burst out laughing. While Rocket thought he was being graceful, he was gallumping around with all the elegance of a flying elephant. Rocket span round spectacularly, then veered dizzily into the rigging. At last he disentangled himself to guffaws from below.

"Stop it, stop this immediately you … you…"

Captain Blood smiled at Ace and gave Swoop his orders. "You will fly up to the top of the mainmast … good … now you look down … yes … and realize that you have forgotten how to fly."

Swoop's loud yell carried over the vampirates' chortles. The fruitbat clutched the swaying mast tightly.

"Now," continued Blood, addressing Rocket. "Your dancing partner has appeared – on that mast. You will dance with him in order to impress the judges – us! The dancing starts now."

A huge roar went up from the crew as they watched Rocket fly upwards and pluck Swoop from the mast. Rocket ignored Swoop's struggles to escape. He grabbed his shoulder and waltzed him in mid-air along the length of the deck. The vampirates cheered and the band began playing faster. Rocket responded by dancing ever more quickly. He threw his reluctant partner high up in the air. Swoop was a tangle of flailing wings and legs. He bounced off the crow's nest and clutched at the sails before Rocket caught him. Rocket span him around the mizzenmast, let go, then grabbed him by the wing-tips.

As the band reached a crescendo of noise, Rocket performed his final manoeuvre. He grasped Swoop and flew cheek to cheek with him. Rocket threw Swoop into three panic-stricken somersaults while he blundered around the rigging and through the mainsail. He swept the canvas off his head and managed to catch his fellow fruitbat just before he plummeted through the deck.

At that moment the music stopped. Rocket

bowed and acknowledged the "applause". Swoop slid to the floor at Ace's feet.

Captain Blood wiped the tears from his eyes. He smiled at Rocket.

"Congratulations, you are a first rate ballet dancer, a tornado. You are to dancing what a bulldozer is to a quiet picnic in the park. You have won the competition and your prize is this delicious cake."

Rocket smiled shyly and took his reward. The "cake" was in fact a rotten onion. Ace's warning shout had no effect. Rocket took a large, happy munch. Abruptly, Captain Blood turned round and headed towards Ace.

"So, now you see what a kind, caring character I am, always thinking of my crew. But our journey is nearly over and I have something else to ask of you and your friends."

The vampirate paused for a second and fixed his gaze upon Ace. "We are nearing Transgoldania. Look into my eyes, it's your turn now…"

Chapter 7

A few hours later, Radar felt someone poking his shoulder. "Wha', wha's a matter?" He blinked through sleepy eyes. When he saw Loopy, the reasons for their voyage came rushing back. "And I'd hoped it was all just a dream," he muttered. "Is everything OK? We're not sinking in the storm are we?"

Once Radar had calmed down, Loopy explained that he had slept through the end of the storm and the following fifteen hours. Radar fell from the ceiling in disbelief. He flew stiffly up on deck where he breathed in the sea breeze. "My head aches," he groaned. "So do my bones, and my mouth feels like it's covered with kiwi fruit skin. I'm not sure I'm ready for the vampirates yet. Where are they by the way?"

"If my chart reading is up to scratch," answered Loopy. "They're dead ahead."

Radar began to feel even worse. He took the offered binoculars and focused in the direction Loopy was pointing. A dark island jumped out at him. Sharp thistles and nettles clung grimly to the inhospitable rock, strangling any other plants that dared grow nearby. The base of the island was obscured by clouds of spray thrown up by waves beating themselves against the cliffs. Radar imagined the rocks tearing through their wooden hull and shivered – he wouldn't like to be shipwrecked here.

"It certainly looks like Transgoldania but where's Port o' Plunder?" said Radar, scanning the island. "We'll sail around the island but don't get any closer to shore. Once we find the port we'll moor out of sight and watch from a distance."

Loopy looked disappointed. "OK, OK. I'll steer to starboard."

Radar sat in the bows, expecting the boat to turn away … but they carried on towards the island. "What's happening?" he asked.

"Haul in the mainsail, take down the spin-naker, jib to the left." A stream of commands came from Loopy. A roaring sound filled Radar's ears. He saw a wall of surf ahead.

"What are you doing?" he yelled.

"We're caught in a rip-tide. I can't steer out of it, hang on."

Radar clung to the mast grimly. The boat picked up speed as it was caught in the tide and sucked towards the island. Salt water poured over the decks. The boat lurched into the trough of the wave and listed to starboard. Radar heard rocks scraping the keel. He turned round to see Loopy struggling to hold the tiller, unaware of a wall of water that was bearing down on them.

"Look ou—" he yelled. His warning was drowned out by the wave. Loopy disappeared from sight as it broke just behind them. The boat was pushed forwards at an incredible speed, its bows dipped lower and lower … then suddenly it was hurled out from the churning sea into calm water. Radar dashed over to find Loopy. There was no sign of her by the tiller – she surfaced from the crow's nest, where she had been thrown by the force of the wave.

"That was a lucky escape," she grinned.

"I'm not so sure," gulped Radar. "Look around."

Loopy's eyes opened wide in amazement. They were floating inside an enormous cavern. At the far end, the tides had carved a horseshoe bay out of solid rock. Eroded rocks formed a protective harbour wall inside which *The Black Fang* was moored. Lining the dockside were a series of large wooden statues. The vampirates' ship was tied up against one. With a gulp Loopy realized what they were: they were trophies – the figure-heads of ships captured in battle.

Three small buildings for ship and sail repairs were dotted along the docks. Towering high above them was a huge castle that had been built on the top of sheer cliffs overlooking the port. Castle Blood was vast. A jumble of different shaped towers thrust their way above the battlements. Parts of the outer wall had collapsed, allowing glimpses inside of stern stone buildings and ivy-covered walls. Spiky turrets and gruesome gargoyles stood guard over the main gates. Arrow slits kept watch while sharp spikes bristled out from the ramparts. A series of ropes and pulleys connected the castle to the docks below. Radar and Loopy looked at each other. They had escaped the treacherous tide but it had washed them up right inside Port o' Plunder. The vampirates' base was situated inside the cave to protect them from sunlight.

"WOW," breathed Loopy. "It's awesome."

"It's awful, more like," replied Radar. "Let's get out of here."

Loopy stopped him in mid-flight. They couldn't leave the cave until the tide had turned. "OK, well in that case we'll moor behind this rock. I just hope the vampirates haven't spotted us already."

Loopy reluctantly moored the boat while Radar kept a close watch on the castle. It looked as though they had been lucky, no one had seen them.

"We'll just stay and wait," he said. "This is near enough."

"No, it isn't," Loopy replied. "It seems a shame to have come this far and not get a really good look. Let's go closer."

"But you said…"

"I said I wanted to watch the action. I didn't

say where from. Stay here if you want, I'm off."

And with that she was gone. Radar sat in the gently rocking boat, thoughts racing. It was typical. Loopy was going to get herself caught – well, let her. That would teach her a lesson. Radar shivered. He looked over his shoulder. What was that noise? Was it a vampirate sneaking up on him? No, it was just some driftwood banging against the hull. Radar hugged himself and stared into the dark water. A pair of black eyes stared back at him – a shark was circling the boat. The sound of water trickling and dripping and lapping filled his ears. Rocks took on strange monstrous shapes that seemed to be moving towards him.

"Wait for me, I'm coming with you," Radar hissed and he launched himself after Loopy.

"I'm glad you came along," she said once Radar had caught her up. "What made you change your mind?"

"Oh, I thought you might need some

looking after," replied Radar, crossing his fingers. "Is this near enough for you?"

"Just a few flaps further." By now they were flying high above *The Black Fang*. Near the docks, at the bottom of the cliff, Radar spotted movement. Ropes creaking, pulleys squeaking, a group of vampirates led by Bo'sun Bones were hauling a huge, cylindrical object up the cliff towards the castle. It was a giant cannon! Radar wondered why they were going to all that effort to hoist it into the castle. There was no time to think up an answer as he tried to catch up with his cousin.

"A little bit closer." Now they were so close to the castle they could make out the faces on the snarling gargoyles that jutted out from the walls.

"And seeing as we've got this far – let's go in." And with that Loopy darted down to the highest turret in the castle and flew in through an open window. She did it so quickly that she didn't hear Radar's warning squeak; nor did she notice the wire she brushed on her way in. Radar saw Loopy's legs disappear, then the window slammed shut and he heard a rumbling sound. Suddenly he was alone. Hoarse shouts and the beating of wings echoed from the castle. Radar flew for cover.

Chapter 8

Loopy stared around at her prison. As soon as she had flown through the window it had shut behind her while a cage had crashed down from the ceiling and imprisoned her behind bars. She was in an alcove in the corner of a strangely-shaped room. Her eye was caught by the unusual objects dotted around.

A stuffed crocodile hung from the ceiling while scorpions stalked round a nearby glass cage. Deadly-looking weapons and nautical nick-nacks were nailed to the walls and covered the surface of a large desk. Behind the desk was a leather armchair. As Loopy watched, it swung around revealing a smiling vampirate. Loopy sprang back to the far end of the cage. The hat, the smile that was scarier than a sword – it could only be Captain Blood!

"And what have we caught here?" Loopy's blood froze in her veins. "A pathetic solitary fruitbat, hardly a fine catch for a captain's table. Is this the finest specimen Fruit Isle has to offer? I must confess I was expecting something better than a mere girl."

Loopy scowled. He was just like Ace. The vampirate continued in a voice that, although quiet, contained steely menace.

"I suppose you were going to rescue your friends… Well, it is of no importance as they will be free soon. So long as your fellow bats stick to their side of the bargain I will stick to mine, my word of honour."

"Word of dishonour more like," Loopy was

about to add. She stopped herself in time but it made no difference, Captain Blood seemed to read her mind.

"Ah, trust! Something that is so lacking in this world. But I know that you believe me." The vampirate concentrated his gaze upon Loopy. "And now, by the clicking of my fangs it's time some trickery began. You will trust me, trust me … trust me."

Loopy stared at Captain Blood. His eyes were burrowing inside her head, the words zeroed in to her brain. She tried to struggle with them. "I cannot trust him … can't trust … can't trust…"

Loopy felt herself weakening. The world outside seemed to shrink and focus on the room. As the words echoed inside her head, Loopy heard a distant clock. It struck ten times, jerking a distant part of Loopy's mind into consciousness. She remembered why she was in the vampirates' castle and she remembered that, at midnight tonight, *The Golden*

Apple would be sailing into Port o' Plunder.

In a flash Loopy realized that Captain Blood was trying to hypnotize her and that he certainly could not be trusted. She also realized that she mustn't let him know he had been rumbled. Loopy let her eyes glaze over and her head droop.

Captain Blood looked pleased. He stood up and talked almost pleasantly.

"Now you are under my control. You will stay hypnotized unless I say the words 'revenge is sweet'. When the right time comes, your task will be to wave happily to the crew of *The Golden Apple* and to make them relax by telling them how well I have treated you."

The vampirate rubbed his hands with glee then continued: "You certainly chose a marvellous place to enter my castle. This is my own special tower. It has a wonderful view over the bay. I've cleared the next room to have a new toy installed – I've called it the

Avenger. If you're lucky you may see what it can do. I intend to have a small portrait painted of my latest victory. You may see the frame but I doubt you will ever see the finished picture."

He broke off, chuckling, leant over and rang a ship's bell.

"All that remains from a little skirmish," he informed Loopy.

The sad tolling of the bell had scarcely finished echoing through the tower when two burly vampirates appeared.

"Take her away," Captain Blood ordered. "Regrettably, you will be staying in one of my dungeons. It's for your own safety, you understand, some of my crew can hardly resist a fresh supply of blood." The captain turned to the guards. "Make sure all the fruit-bats are carefully watched. They must not escape."

Loopy flew down the tower's spiral stair-case. A series of portraits were hanging on the walls. All of them had gold frames with skulls at each corner and each showed vampirates in action through the ages. Loopy remembered Aunt Bathilda's ancestor portraits; these must be Captain Blood's. But when she looked closely she noticed that the main figure in them looked exactly the same. How could that be?

At that moment a hearty bellow came from high above.

"So now you've seen me through the centuries. When you live as long as I have, you don't have many ancestors."

Captain Blood's guffaws followed Loopy through the castle. She was led through long draughty corridors and down narrow steps. Each level of the castle seemed danker and dingier than the next. Loopy was shivering by the time a thick door was unlocked and she was pushed into a cold, draughty dungeon.

"Oww!" Loopy dusted cobwebs off her face before realizing she was not alone in the dungeon. "Ace, Swoop, Rocket! How are you?"

Rocket acted first. He carefully put a rotten onion in his pocket then raced up to Loopy.

"At last," he smiled. "A proper dancing partner."

Before Loopy could react she was being foxtrotted at high speed through the cell.

"Hey, get off, you big lunk, let me go," she protested. "This is not the time for stupid dances."

Sulkily, Rocket did as he was told, complaining. "You're no fun. I shall just have to find someone who appreciates my delicate skill."

"What's got into him? Is he OK?" Loopy asked Swoop. "Hold on a second. Why are you crouched on the floor?"

"D … don't touch me," Swoop quavered. "I'm staying where I'm happy – on the ground. I can't fly."

"What the…?" Loopy suddenly saw the far-away look in Swoop's eyes and realized he had been hypnotized. As Rocket picked Swoop up and began throwing him through the air she knew that Blood had got Rocket too. That only left Ace. At least he was behaving normally. "Come on. We've got to get out of here quickly. What plans have you made?"

"Plans?" echoed Ace blankly.

"Yes, we haven't got much time. Maybe we could trick the guards by pretending one of us is ill – not that that's very far from the truth. When the guards investigate, we rush them and escape."

"Escape?" replied Ace. "ESCAPE! Call the guards, there's an escape plan. Lock her up, she mentioned escape. Guards, guards!" Ace imitated the sound of a fire engine's siren and began hammering on the door.

"Shut up," hissed Loopy. Ace dodged her attempted grab and continued banging. The guards would be there soon. Captain Blood must have hypnotized Ace to warn his crew of any escape. She couldn't stop him. Luckily Rocket did! He was practising one of his more acrobatic dance manoeuvres. He threw Swoop in the air and missed his catch. Swoop scored a direct hit on Ace.

"Phew!" Silence reigned in the dungeon and Loopy bit her lip. The others were hopeless. They had obviously all been hypnotized by Captain Blood. Her brain raced. She didn't know exactly what the vampirate was planning but she knew it would be bad for the fruitbats. They had to escape – although the state the others were in would make it very difficult. Unless she could get them to snap out of it they would have to rely on Radar. Loopy wondered where he was and what he was doing now…

At that moment Radar was trying to keep very still. After Loopy's capture, hordes of vampirates had darkened the sky. They had poured out of the castle and from *The Black*

Fang, cutting off Radar's escape route out of the port.

Radar had flown for his life. He had swooped around the castle, darting behind drains and loose bricks before landing, breathlessly, on a patch of level ground outside the castle walls. Statues and strange stone boxes dotted the area. Some of them were tumbling down, all of them were overgrown with tangles of dark ivy and cobwebs.

A creaking of wood and hoarse orders warned Radar of trouble. He dragged himself behind one of the stone boxes as a group of vampirates, led by Bo'sun Bones, landed a few metres away. They were still hoisting the cannon up the cliff. Radar tried to melt into the crumbling stonework. His heart was pounding so loudly he was sure the others would hear it, but gradually it slowed down and Radar listened to what the vampirates were saying.

"Only a couple more hours to wait lads, then we'll have some fireworks."

"I hope all this hard work's worth while. Why does the captain want this cannon in his tower anyway?"

"I hope that's not mutinous talk, you swab … Captain Blood had the Avenger built for a special reason. I'll let you into a secret… It's a surprise for those fruitbats when they arrive in port. The captain's got the hostages all lined up so they'll wave from the battlements. The crew will suspect nothing. He's going to wait until the treasure's unloaded from *The Golden Apple*, then he'll attack. One shot from this beauty should sink them… Now, to work. Put your backs into it. There's double grog rations for everyone once it's done. *Heave ho and up she rises, heave ho and up she rises, heave ho and up she rises, early in the evening*."

The vampirates took the strain. Gradually the cannon was hauled up into the air, leaving Radar on the plateau alone. *Alone*. Radar had never felt so alone. He was leagues away from home, feeling ill, with the future of Fruit Isle depending on him. Captain Blood was obviously not going to stick to his side of the bargain; *The Golden Apple* was sailing into a trap. The vampirate's revenge would be complete – and what stood in his way? Radar!

Not for the first time, Radar wished he had stayed at home. What could he do? The entrance to the port was heavily guarded but he might just be able to reach the batamaran and sail out to warn the crew of *The Golden Apple*. Or, if he could find a way into the castle and rescue the Fruit Gang, then Captain Blood would have no hostages and his plan would be foiled.

Thoughts flashed through Radar's brain. Should he risk rescuing the others? If Loopy had listened to him, she would never have got caught. And as for the others, they had followed Ace and he had thrown Radar out of the Fruit Gang.

At last Radar decided. He would show the

Fruit Gang that they had underestimated him. He would rescue them on his own, without any help.

But how could he get into the castle? He needed to get a better look. Radar kicked his way through a thick bush of dripping ivy.

"OWWW!" Radar hopped around until his toe stopped throbbing. He tore away at the green leaves and uncovered a thick stone slab. Words had been carved into it.

Here is Peg-Leg Pete's final mooring place. He survived cannon-balls and cutlass thrusts but it was the woodworm that got him in the end.

Suddenly Radar worked out where he was. He was in a graveyard. The stone box he had been hiding behind was a tomb. He shivered, this was a spooky place. He looked over his shoulder and a carved skull leered at him with sightless eyes. Radar started backwards and nearly fell over a row of headstones.

"Pull yourself together," he muttered. He peered down to read an inscription.

In 1884 vampirate Blackheart fought his last battle. He was a great shipmate and we'll never forget his appetite for battle, booty and blood. Fangs for the memories.

Beside the stone slab was a large square tomb with an overgrown statue and battle scenes carved around the base. Radar cleaned the cobwebs out of the carved inscription with his finger.

Here our shipmate ran aground.
No more shall he raise anchor and upon the
*   seven seas be found.*
He drank too much grog then set sail into fog.
Some said he was barking mad, some said he was
*   just a good old sea dog.*
He was quick on the draw and never one to tarry
But now it's time to rest for Hurricane Harry.

Radar winced, what a terrible poem. It didn't even rhyme very well. Radar repeated it aloud then stopped suddenly. There was something familiar about the inscription. Where had he heard the name, Hurricane Harry, before? Of course, it was in Captain Blood's letter. It had seemed odd then. *"…not even Hurricane Harry will help them escape."*

Could this mean something? Radar's hopes soared. It would be just like Captain Blood to be clever and taunt the fruitbats with a hidden meaning in his letter. Was there some sort of escape route near the tomb? A tunnel perhaps? Radar pulled away the ivy from the statue and began searching for an opening. A few minutes later, he wiped the cobwebs from his wings and hovered above the statue. It was hopeless. He had found nothing. He was going backwards, fast. He had wasted time and was nowhere nearer getting inside the castle. He looked at the statue. More of the captain's words suddenly came back to him.

"I have sworn ... by the hilt of a seadog's cutlass..."

That was it! Radar examined the stone around the hilt of the statue's cutlass. His fingers touched something, something that felt like a button. Radar pressed it and heard a grinding noise. The lid of the tomb was swinging open. After a few moments he cautiously peered inside. A narrow passage led down from the tomb in the direction of the castle. Radar flew round and round with joy. He had done it, he had outsmarted Captain Blood and found a way into his lair. The vampirate thought he had an answer for everything but he had reckoned without Radar. Now it was up to him. It was all up to him.

Radar came back down to earth with a bump. "Keep calm," he muttered to himself. If he could outwit Captain Blood once, he could do it again. He pushed the memory of everything that had gone wrong recently out of his mind in order to steel himself for the challenges ahead. He thought of the vampirates capturing the Fruit Gang and reminded himself of Captain Blood's treachery. Radar clenched his fists. One of them closed around something in his pocket. He pulled it out and saw some of the garlic he had taken from Aunt Bathilda's herb garden. Maybe a larger dose would clear his head and cure him of his flu.

"Desperate times deserve desperate measures," he muttered. Before he could stop himself, he grabbed the garlic and swallowed.

Radar exploded down the tunnel. The tomb lid slammed shut behind, but he didn't even slow down. He headed straight on into the castle. He skidded to a halt at the end of the tunnel where light shone from two circular holes in the wall. Through them he saw a long empty corridor. The coast was clear. Radar found a handle and pushed it and a section of the wall slid silently open. With sweat breaking out on his forehead, Radar flew silently out. It was quiet, very quiet. Danger lay everywhere. He had to keep all his senses alert. A few flaps of the wings took him to a junction. Radar slowed down. He peered round the corner and looked straight into the eyes of a huge vampirate.

"Well shiver me timbers, what have we here, but an intruder. Just when I'm feeling a touch peckish, time for a little bite."

"Hold on, I can explain," quavered Radar. He tried to turn and flee but the vampirate caught him up in seconds. Radar retreated until he could go no further. He was backed up against a suit of armour, his flaps seemed feeble against his huge opponent. He felt his head spinning and only had time to breathe out "HELP!" before fainting. The last thing he saw was a pair of glistening fangs closing in on him…

A loud crash pierced the fog between Radar's ears. He shook his head to clear his sight. He spotted the vampirate lying under a suit of armour. What had happened to him? He didn't want to get too close to find out. He peered at the dazed vampirate and saw blood.

Radar's head began spinning and his wings began to wobble like blancmange. Suddenly he knew why. The realization left him gasping for breath.

"I've been bitten," groaned Radar. "I'm turning into a vampire. These must be the symptoms. There's no hope for me now, it's just a matter of time."

"I wonder how long it will take?" Radar asked himself as he wobbled down the corridor. He looked at his hands – they were white and trembling. His heart began to race. The corridor took him into a long room. Chairs were lined up opposite each other on each side of the long wall. In the middle of the room was a gold mirror frame with skulls at each corner. Radar flew up to it.

"This is it." At first Radar didn't dare look in the mirror but at last he plucked up the courage to do it. "Oh, no," he gasped. He could see the chair and a curtain behind him but not himself. He had no reflection. "It's too late," he wailed. "I'm already a vampirate."

Fingers of fear reached out and clutched his throat. His wings began to tingle. He wondered how long it would be before he started singing sea-chanties and began to crave blood. Radar tried to fight the feeling.

"I can still think like a fruitbat. I must try and help the Fruit Gang before it's too late. I must find them."

Summoning up all his willpower, Radar battled against the dizzy feeling that threatened to swamp him. He took to the air and weaved unsteadily past a rickety chair. He smacked straight into a rusty iron grate in the wall. It gave way under his weight, sending Radar spinning backwards. It's some sort of delivery chute, he realized as he somersaulted into the blackness. Down and round, twisting and turning, Radar bounced from one wall to another. *I wonder where it comes out?* he thought. Up ahead was a patch of light. *I think I'm about to find out.*

Chapter 9

Meanwhile, down in the depths of the castle, Loopy was getting worried. What had happened to Radar? She hoped he was all right. Maybe he had decided to sit it out. He wouldn't know about Blood's plans. Time was running out fast. *The Golden Apple* would soon be sailing into the bay. Little did the crew know that they were sailing into the jaws of a trap. Once they docked in the port, it would snap shut. There would be no way out unless...

"Unless I can esc ... er, get away with you

three." Ace stared at her blankly while Swoop hugged the floor and Rocket performed an airborne *pas de deux*. "Oh, it's hopeless," she groaned. "You're hopeless."

Loopy racked her brains. She had tried everything. Pleading, arguing, shouting – they made no difference. The Fruit Gang wouldn't snap out of it. Swoop wouldn't move, Rocket was tucking into his onion between dancing and Ace was like a zombie unless the E-word was mentioned. Loopy was even beginning to miss arguing with him.

"Think calmly, don't rush," Loopy muttered to herself. "There must be something I can do." She counted to ten, then thought hard. She had once seen a hypnotic show. What had happened? The hypnotist had mesmerized the bats on stage but he had given them a trigger word that would wake them up. Had Captain Blood done the same? Loopy thought back to when the vampirate had tried to cast his spell over her. She had been so busy trying not to pay attention that she could only vaguely remember what he had said. Hold on, there had been something. The captain had spoken a phrase in that dangerous voice of his, now what was it?

"I will be avenged … my revenge is complete…" It was something like that… Suddenly it came flashing back to Loopy. "Revenge is sweet," she squeaked.

Nothing happened. Loopy repeated the words. Again, there was no reaction. She was sure that was the phrase, so what was going wrong? Of course, the voice! The fruitbats would only recognize the trigger words if they were said by Captain Blood – or by someone who sounded like Captain Blood. She had always been good at mimicking voices, especially teachers' – but could she imitate Blood's voice?

She cleared her throat. "Revenge is…" No, that was too high. "Revenge…" No, that was too low. "Reven…" She was getting close.

"Revenge is…" She was nearly there. Trying to keep the nervousness out of her voice, Loopy spoke in a deep, quiet voice. "Revenge is sweet."

The far-away look in the fruitbats' eyes suddenly disappeared. The trio shook their heads and gazed around the dungeon as if they were waking up from a deep sleep.

"What's occurring, flyers?" Swoop stretched out his wings and took to the air. "I need to catch some thermals. I've just had a most unhappy nightmare."

"Me too!" said Rocket. He looked in disgust at the rotten onion in his hand. "Yeeeuch!"

Ace tried to cover up his confusion when he saw Loopy.

"Hey, look what the cat dragged in. What are you doing here?"

"Charmed, I'm sure," Loopy replied. "Maybe I should have left you hypnotized."

"Hypnotized? That sort of mumbo jumbo wouldn't work on me," Ace replied. "What are you talking about? How did we get here? What's going on?"

"I don't think you'd believe me if I told you," answered Loopy. "But I hope you will believe me when I tell you about Captain Blood's piratical plans."

By the time she had explained what she knew, the others were back to normal.

"We can't let him get away with it," Ace thundered. "The devious, dastardly, double-crossing devil. We must get away."

At last, thought Loopy. We're agreeing on something. Aloud, she asked the others a question. "So who's got any ideas on how we can escape?"

She smiled at the puzzled look that crossed Ace's face as he found himself standing in front of the dungeon door at the mention of the word "escape". Ace crossed his wings and looked thoughtful. "I know, we'll use the old fake illness plan," he stated.

"Hey, that was my idea," Loopy said.

"Give it a rest, you two," Swoop interrupted. "What's this fake illness lark?"

Ace quietly explained the idea. After a few moments the fruitbats all understood their roles. They took up positions. Ace began hammering on the door and yelling. "Help, help. Guard! Rocket's in agony. It must have been something he's eaten."

A vampirate appeared outside the door. He peered through the grate and saw Rocket doubled up on the floor.

"Please help him," pleaded Ace.

"Oh, no," hissed the guard. "The captain told me to keep the hostages healthy." He unlocked the door and dashed in. As he did so, he heard a whistle from up above and saw Swoop hovering above him, a bucket in his hands. "But ... but you're supposed to be hypnotized," stuttered the guard.

At that moment, Swoop dropped the bucket on the guard's head, Loopy grabbed his keys and the four fruitbats flew out of the dungeon. They locked the door behind them.

"We did it," grinned Rocket. "That was easy." The fruitbats turned away from the dungeon – and stopped dead in their tracks.

Ten more vampirates were right in front of them.

"It's just as well we were here too," grinned one of them. "The penthouse not good enough for you, eh? Trying to escape, were you? Well, go ahead and try."

The fruitbats looked at each other, then at the vampirates. The vampirates were armed to the teeth and had drawn their cutlasses. It was looking grim for the fruitbats. "It'll take a miracle to get us out of this," Loopy muttered to herself.

At that moment Radar burst on to the scene. He appeared in a blur of somersaults through a narrow opening high up on the wall and landed amongst the vampirates, sending them crashing and spinning into the walls.

"What the…" The fruitbats were almost as

dazed as the vampirates by this sudden apparition. Was this really Radar? Ace could hardly believe his eyes when he saw Radar bounce off the stomach of a burly vampirate, draw a cutlass and with the yell "Bat Attack!" charge after the guards. The vampirates fled in terror.

"R ... Radar, is that you, what's happening?"

"There's very little time left," boomed the reply. Radar related what he had overheard Bo'sun Bones saying. Loopy clenched her fist; her suspicions about Captain Blood had been right all along. That explained the vampirate's plans, but what was the explanation for the change in Radar?

"Keep back, stay away from me," replied Radar, his voice cracking with emotion. "It's all over. I was bitten by a vampirate. He bit me, then collapsed. I checked in a mirror in the Great Hall. I have no reflection, I am turning into a vampirate. It's only a matter of time before I start craving fresh blood and develop a taste for pirate plunder. You must go now and warn the others... Remember me how I was. Go, my head is spinning, it must be taking over..."

Rocket looked at Radar in horror. "What are we waiting for? Let's get out of here."

"I agree," nodded Ace. "We mustn't waste this chance."

"So long, old buddy," Swoop gulped. "Isn't there anything we can do?"

"Hold on a second." Loopy's voice stopped the trio in their tracks. "Where were you bitten?"

"In a corridor upstairs," came the reply. Radar paused. "Oh ... I see, I was bitten on the neck."

"But you're wearing Aunt Bathilda's scarf. Her knitting's like chain mail, even a vampirate's fangs couldn't get through that. Show us the bite mark."

With a trembling hand, Radar took off the scarf and bared his neck. There was no sign of a bite. "But, but how can that be? What about the mirror?"

"Why would there be a mirror in a vampirate's castle when we know they don't have a reflection? Hold on, was the frame around this mirror gold with skulls at each side?" Radar nodded and Loopy smiled.

"That wasn't a mirror, that was a picture frame. Captain Blood is waiting to put his latest portrait into it. You just looked through it, no wonder you didn't see a reflection."

"But … but I still don't think we should take any chances. You haven't explained the symptoms. What could have caused them?" Ace interrupted.

"Elementary, my dear Ace." Loopy was beginning to enjoy this. She turned to Radar. "The symptoms sound the same as when you had some of Aunt Bathilda's cake. Have you eaten anything similar since?"

Of course, the garlic! Radar felt a huge weight lift off his shoulders. It was OK, he wasn't going to become a vampirate after all. Then his smile froze on his lips. Did that mean that all his swashbuckling antics had been dangerous after all? He could have been killed. Radar's knees began to buckle and the contents of his stomach swashed about.

"You've gone very white, Radar. Are you OK? Thanks for rescuing us, you did brilliantly. Boy, were we pleased to see you."

"You were?" Radar did his best to cover up his surprise. Inside his heart was racing with excitement. He had done it. He had rescued all the others on his own, without any help. "Well, of course. Anyone would have done the same."

"The only thing that I can't figure out is why the vampirate didn't bite you and what knocked him out."

Radar shrugged. He wasn't bothered by that, he wanted to savour his moment of triumph. Unfortunately the moment didn't last. Ace drew himself up to his full height and tried to take charge.

"Now we're out of that dungeon it's time to let an escape expert take over."

"And I suppose you think you are that expert?" Loopy popped some gum in her mouth and began chewing. "And you expect us to listen to your plan when a few minutes ago you couldn't escape your way out of a paper bag?"

"Now hold on," began Ace. "As leader and master strategist, I expect my plan to be followed. What we are going to do is this…"

He broke off as he was interrupted by the sound of a bell clanging. "There's no more time to waste. That's an alarm bell. Our escape's been discovered."

"Or it could be a signal to say that *The Golden Apple*'s in sight," Loopy said defiantly.

"Hey, chill out you two," interrupted Swoop. "Whatever it means, it means we've got to get our skates on. Come on!"

The fruitbats winged their way up and out of the dungeons. Through the maze of hallways and corridors they sped until they found themselves in a great hall. A huge chandelier hung from the tall ceiling and three sets of double doors led off in different directions. Which way now?

"Uh-oh," groaned Radar, glancing at Loopy and Ace. "I can sense trouble brewing."

Radar was right but not in the way he meant. Before the fruitbats could move, the doors burst open and a horde of vampirates appeared, led by Mr Leech and Bo'sun Bones.

Chapter 10

The silence was broken by Mr Leech.

"It looks like we arrived just in time," he hissed. "Captain Blood was wondering when the little one with glasses would turn up. It was a brave attempt at a rescue. However, the captain would be angry if his plans were sunk without trace and you wouldn't like to see the captain when he's angry. Bo'sun Bones, weapons please."

"It'll be my pleasure," replied the bo'sun. He produced cutlasses and daggers from his pockets. They flashed through the air and were caught by the vampirates. Bo'sun Bones chuckled and danced a jig in celebration.

The fruitbats looked at the motley crew surrounding them. Radar's brain raced.

"We'll only win this battle if we're all fighting together," he muttered. "What do you say, Ace? Will the Fruit Gang fly together again?"

Ace nodded and shook Radar's hand.

"What about me? Not that I'm interested in joining – not until I receive my apologies," Loopy said. Before she could get a reply the vampirates launched their attack. Screaming blood-curdling yells, they charged.

"Stand by to repel attackers," yelled Ace. The first vampirate lunged at Swoop with his cutlass. Swoop soared above the sword stroke, then landed SMACK straight on his attacker's head. Gathering the still spinning sword from the dazed villain, he flew off again. In one fluid movement he arced above the vampirates' heads and sliced through the ropes holding the iron chandelier. It crashed down amongst the attackers, sending them flying ... straight into a volley of rotten onion fired by Rocket.

"Five down, twenty to go," grinned Rocket, giving Swoop the thumbs up. "I'm beginning to enjoy this."

"First blood to us," Loopy muttered. "But I don't think they're going to stop there."

She was right. The vampirates regrouped. Mr Leech shouted out new orders.

"Bite on sight, take no prisoners." A clicking noise carried through the hall as pairs of sharp white fangs glinted in the darkness.

"Retreat," hissed Ace urgently. "We've got to get some weapons or we've no chance." He grabbed Swoop's sword and pushed the others out of a door.

The fruitbats formed into an arrow formation. With Swoop at the tip and Ace acting as rearguard, the fruitbats took off. Staying a few flaps ahead of their pirate pursuers, the fruitbats flew through the castle. Into a tall

...ber with a vaulted ceiling they raced. A large fireplace dominated the far end while long tables and cupboards were scattered about the room. Rocket smiled.

"This must be the kitchen."

"And this is where we would have ended up," Radar gulped. "On those plates."

Rocket's grin vanished. So had Ace. He resurfaced from inside a cupboard brandishing a heavy saucepan.

"Grab these pans and ladles and things," he hissed. "They'll do as weapons ... that's it ... look out!"

Bo'sun Bones and his crew had arrived. Instantly, the kitchen was full of bats ducking, darting and wheeling. Using the pans and ladles as weapons, the fruitbats held their attackers at bay. Metallic clunks and clangs echoed off the stone walls. A hail of saucepan lid frisbees, thrown by Swoop, knocked unwary vampirates out of the sky.

"We can't hold them for ever. Quick, let's go."

The fivesome swerved their way out by a small opening. Down and down they flew into a cold, musty room.

"This is my lucky day," Rocket grinned. "We're in the drinks cellar."

"There's no time for enjoying it," Loopy said. "Smash the bottles and the barrels. That should slow them up."

The fruitbats heard howls of anger as they dived out of the cellar. Rocket dropped his bottle and bounced from wall to wall as they flew up and round a spiral staircase. Cold air hit them as they surged outside. They flew up out of the castle's main building and along the battlements. Cannons were lined up on platforms, all aiming out to sea – and at *The Golden Apple*, which was just entering the cavern. The fruitbats knocked the cannon-balls off the walls.

Up ahead was a large tower with thick studded doors and barred windows. Rocket, Swoop, Loopy and Radar swept on past it

...us the gate house. Ace gazed inside the tower and saw cannonballs, cutlasses and barrels of gunpowder – it was the vampirates' arsenal. If they could get inside and wreck the weapons, the vampirates would be harm-less.

"Come back," Ace yelled. "We've got to get inside here."

The fruitbats turned back. Loopy's eyes lit up at what she saw.

"Wow, all we need is a light to blow the whole place upside down."

"If we do that we'll all blow up," gulped Radar.

"Well said. What we need is water – if we dampen the gunpowder it'll be useless." Ace and Loopy glared at each other.

"Look out!" warned Swoop. "Bandits ten o'clock."

The bandits were led by Leech and Bones. They launched a two-pronged attack, flying round from either side of the tower, driving a wedge between the fruitbats, cutting them off from each other.

"Re-form everyone," ordered Ace. "Get back into formation."

The flying battle filled the skies. Heavily outnumbered, the fruitbats swerved around the tower. They dodged the pirates' cutlass swipes and jinked over battlements as they attempted to regroup. The fight swayed and moved from one side to another. The vampirates had the advantage in numbers but the fruitbats were not going to give up without a struggle.

Two huge vampirates lumbered towards Loopy from either side. One of them flexed his tattooed arms and grinned a toothy smile.

"This should be easy," he hissed. "Get her!" Loopy held her ground then, at the last moment, took off. The vampirates clutched solid air then collided with each other. Loopy looped-the-loop. On the way

___, she whipped out an iron ladle and __UNK, CLUNK, the vampirates slid to the floor.

"Now who's in trouble?" muttered Loopy. She instinctively looked for Radar, but it was Ace who needed help. Mr Leech had targeted him specifically and was using his extra reach to get closer and closer to the fruitbat. Ace was weakening as he fended off each crashing cutlass thrust. At last, the vampirate dashed the saucepan from his hand. Ace yelled out as Mr Leech caught him in a vice-like grip.

Loopy desperately fought her way through the vampirates towards him. Using her ladle, she clonked three vampirates who spiralled down to the ground.

"Nearly there, nearly there." Loopy could see the pink scars on Mr Leech, she could see the veins standing out on his arm and the knuckles tightening over Ace. His teeth glistened with anticipation. Loopy raised her

ladle, shouting, "Oh, no you don't …
OWWW!"

At the last minute, Leech had stretched out
his arm and caught her in mid-swipe. Loopy
wriggled helplessly as Leech pulled Ace
closer. She was only a few centimetres away
but it might as well be a kilometre. She was
being held so tightly that she couldn't move
any closer or bash her opponent. She watched
in horror. Ace was only millimetres away
from being the vampirate's latest victim.
There was nothing she could do.

Or was there? Loopy began chewing
furiously. It might just work, if I time it right,
she thought. She took a deep breath and blew.
The vampirate opened his mouth greedily,
threw back his head then bit … straight into
a chewing gum bubble!

The bubble burst, splattering Mr Leech's
face with sticky goo.

"What the…?" The vampirate yelled in surprise. Dropping the two fruitbats he tried to

unstick his jaws. But each time he tried to chew his way through the gum, he got himself more and more wrapped up. At last, his mouth was completely gummed up. "Mnnnn, mnnnn."

Loopy saw their chance. She flew a breathless Ace up and over the tower, where they almost collided with Swoop and Rocket.

"Is Ace OK?" asked Rocket. "What happened…?"

"Loopy saved me," Ace gasped between gulps of air. "Thank you! I was wrong, I'm sorry."

"It was nothing," replied Loopy, smiling. "You'd have done the same."

"I hate to interrupt this touching moment," Rocket winced, fending off another airborne assault. "But have you seen Radar?"

There he was! Bo'sun Bones had cornered Radar and backed him up against the tower wall. Between him and the fruitbats was a solid line of vampirates. They could only watch in horror.

"Uh, oh," Radar gulped as he felt sharp, cold stones sticking into his back. There were no secret passages to help him this time. Then he remembered what he had picked up from the kitchen. He waited until the bo'sun lunged, then whipped out … a kettle! He desperately threw it at his opponent but the bo'sun easily ducked out of its way.

"Oh, dear," Bo'sun Bones sighed sarcastically. "That is a shame." He rubbed his hands and waved away the other vampirates. "Still, seeing that kettle has made me feel quite thirsty. I feel like a drink, a quick nip of something. A jug of blood perhaps – or should that be a jugular of blood?"

Radar's eyes opened wide. Bo'sun Bones's ugly mug filled his line of vision. Radar tried to move but his nose started to twitch and his whole body tensed up. "Aaah … aah … attischoo," Radar sneezed in the bo'sun's face.

The vampirate flew backwards as if he had been struck by a shaft of sunlight.

"Get away," he yelled. "Get back everyone. His breath … he's been eating garlic."

Garlic! Garlic! It scared away vampirates. Radar couldn't believe his luck. As Bo'sun Bones turned to flee, Radar delved into his pockets and pulled out a clove of garlic. It was the last one. "Down the hatch," he said, taking a quick crunch, then charged. The ring of steel that surrounded him melted away. He flew over to join the others.

The fruitbats had temporarily gained the advantage. Seeing Bones and Leech beaten, their crew had retreated to lick their wounds and were hovering above the arsenal.

"So what do we do now? Attack the tower or retreat to *The Golden Apple*?"

"I think we retreat," Loopy said. Radar held his breath. Would the truce between Loopy and Ace last?

"OK, OK, I'll follow."

"Phew!" Radar breathed a sigh of relief. He slipstreamed behind the others. They slipped back into the arrow formation and darted between turrets. Up ahead they could see *The Golden Apple*. It was slowly sailing through the bay towards the harbour. Just in front of them was the gate house. Swoop spotted vampirates hovering above the building. Quickly they peeled away and headed through it.

There's freedom, Radar thought to himself. We're nearly out of the castle, just a few more flaps and we've escaped. At last, we've done it. Nothing can stop us now…

CRASH, RATTLE, CLUNK. A metal grid slammed down in front of Radar. THUD! When he opened his eyes again, he saw the other fruitbats looking down at him. "I'm OK. What happened?"

"Bo'sun Bones cut the rope securing the portcullis," Swoop explained. "We're stuck."

"I guess this is what you call a dead end," Rocket added bitterly. "Look!"

Radar peered back the way they had flown, back through the gate house and into the castle. There were Bo'sun Bones and Mr Leech. Beside them was a loaded cannon that was pointing directly into the gate house.

Had they come so far only to be beaten within sight of safety? Swoop tried to squeeze through the portcullis – the holes were too small. Rocket strained to lift the portcullis – it was too heavy to budge. Ace and Loopy stared at the solid walls surrounding them and racked their brains. It was no good, they were trapped, the only way out was covered by the vampirates' cannon. After a few seconds the fruitbats looked at each other sadly. This was it! There was no escape this time. The vampirates had outsmarted them. They would have the last laugh after all.

Mr Leech struck a match and lit the three torches Bo'sun Bones had magicked out of his pockets.

"Let's see your garlic ward this off. We're going to blow you sky-high with a broadside you won't forget. And once we've done that, we'll load our other guns and train them on *The Golden Apple*."

"You've led us a merry dance through the castle," sneered the bo'sun, effortlessly juggling the flaming brands. "Although not so merry as the one we saw on *The Black Fang*."

The three lighted torches hovered dangerously near the cannon's fuse, then they lit the short piece of rope. It sparked its way towards the barrel of the cannon while the bo'sun continued. "Yes, the only dancing competition you'll win is one for belly dancing – bulldozer."

Huge guffaws bellowed out from the vampirates. Loopy and Radar looked at each other in astonishment. What were the gruesome twosome talking about? Ace looked confused, but the vampirates' speech triggered something in the back of Swoop and Rocket's minds. A far-off distant memory – blurred images of flying and falling … of laughter and collapsing. Swoop's eyes narrowed into angry slits. The vampirates had made a fool of him before, now he would show them. Rocket roared with anger. He would teach them to mess with him. They both exploded into action!

Swoop switched to turbo-fly and blasted straight towards the barrel of the gun. Rocket put his head down and charged. He bull-dozed two vampirates out of the way and knocked three others up into the air. Swoop grabbed one of them by his bandanna, span him round and sent him spinning towards the cannon. The vampirate careered into the base of the gun. It lurched around in a semi-circle then it went off. The cannonball flew through the air, crashed through a window and landed … in the tower where the vampirates' weapons were stored!

Silence descended for a moment while the fruitbats and the vampirates watched the tower. Then an enormous bang shattered the stillness. Flames burst out of each window.

The roof blew out and stones whistled through the air. Bo'sun Bones and Mr Leech gulped. They were so shocked they couldn't move. The fruitbats saw their chance.

"We've done it," yelled Rocket. "Come on, we may still be in time!"

The fruitbats whooshed back out of the gate house and headed for safety. Behind them, flames roared and gunpower exploded. The vampirates began fetching buckets of water from the castle well. They were so busy trying to put out the fire that they had no time to pursue the five fruitbats. Swoop led the way as they flew over a courtyard, dodging stray cannonballs and pieces of flaming masonry that were hurled out from the blazing tower.

Up ahead was the last wall. All they had to do was fly over it and reach *The Golden Apple*. Surely they were free now. The wall was the final obstacle, nothing could stop them…

"Ha, ha, ha!" A wild howl of laughter made

the hair on the back of their necks stand on end. It was followed by a familiar voice that boomed out, "You have come this far, but you will go no further. My revenge will not be thwarted. If you thought you could outwit me then you have another thought coming. So far you have only dealt with those fools. Now it is time to face Captain Blood."

Before the five small fruitbats could react, a huge shadow darkened the courtyard. Slowly, smoothly, floating towards them was Captain Blood!

Chapter 11

The fruitbats looked at each other in horror as their old enemy advanced remorselessly upon them, cape billowing behind him. They had beaten the other vampirates but Captain Blood was a different proposition altogether. He was bound to stop them unless they stuck together. The fruitbats all seemed to have the same idea.

"Close up formation," yelled Ace.

"Get ready to go on the command," Loopy added.

Captain Blood chuckled. "You foolish

fruitbats, you will never defeat me."

"Come on, we've just got to get over the wall. Don't stop for anything. Bat attack!"

As the fruitbats accelerated, the captain beamed. He whipped out a blunderbuss from under his cape and pointed it at the fruitbats.

"I think I'll just wing you – a flesh wound perhaps, one that produces a lot of blood." He licked his lips and pulled the trigger.

"Yikes!" yelled Radar. "Scatter."

The fruitbats peeled away, up, down, left and right as the bullet exploded in their midst. They were blown out of control and sent spinning off in every direction. There was no time to regroup. Their plan to stick together was in tatters, it was every bat for him or herself.

Rocket found himself somersaulting over the castle walls. Smoke and flames were billowing from the sails of *The Black Fang*. A stray cannonball must have hit it. Its crew members were frantically trying to put out the fire; they didn't spot Rocket hovering above them. He saw *The Golden Apple* just outside the harbour. He would soon reach it unless Captain Blood was after him. Not daring to look back, he flew like the wind. Seconds later he was joined by Swoop. They looked at each other. What had happened to the others?

Ace had been blown sideways through an arrow slit into a tall tower. He landed on a stone staircase. He heard a wing brushing the wall below and roared up the stairs. On the first landing he nearly collided with Loopy.

"Thank goodness it's you," he breathed. "I thought it was the captain."

"So did I," Loopy said, putting her ladle away. "Have you seen the others?"

Ace shook his head but there was no time to hang about. The duo flew up through the tower past familiar portraits. Ace spotted an open window. He was just about to fly out when Loopy stopped him. She remembered Captain Blood's room at the top of the tower and what Radar had overheard. Suddenly she realized that they had overlooked something. Even if they reached *The Golden Apple* they would be in trouble. She turned to Ace and whispered in his ear.

Ace went pale. "You're right," he said. "OK, let's go."

A minute later the duo launched themselves out of the tower. They blazed a trail over the harbour and landed on *The Golden Apple* without any problems. The decks were packed with fruitbats. Some were cheering their safe return while others were trying to obey shouted orders to turn the ship around.

Swoop appeared from amongst the sails and Rocket's head popped up from behind some food barrels.

"We did it," yelled Ace excitedly, clapping Rocket on the back. Loopy smiled until a dark shadow fell over her.

"Oh, Aunt B. Er, I can explain," she began then trailed off.

"You certainly have a great deal of explaining to do. I am only grateful that Radar was not so stupid as to be lured out here."

The colour drained from Loopy's face. If Aunt Bathilda didn't think Radar was with them, she must not have seen him. So where was he? She yelled to the others. Had they seen him? Where was Radar? At that moment a loud crash echoed through the cave. Flames leapt up from somewhere inside the castle, lighting up the entire scene.

"Look, there's the way out."

"And there's Radar," whispered Loopy.

The fruitbats turned to look where Loopy was pointing. On the castle's battlements, silhouetted in the blood red glare were two figures – Radar and Captain Blood!

"Oh, no," groaned Ace. "I might have known Radar would get himself caught. He's Blood's hostage now."

"It's put me right off my food," Rocket added.

"What can we do? Is there any way of rescuing him?"

"I don't think so, Swoop," Loopy replied. "There's only one person who can save the day now – and that's Radar. It's up to him."

She squinted up at the two figures on the battlements and willed Radar to win. *Come on*, she thought. *I don't know how Captain Blood captured you, but I know you can beat him.*

Radar gulped as he looked down at *The Golden Apple* below. The blast from Captain Blood's blunderbuss had blown him sky high. He had gone straight up into the air and then plummeted down on to the stony castle floor. By the time he had cleared his senses, a large figure was blocking his view. Captain Blood was staring down at him. There was no escape. *Why me?* Radar wailed to himself.

Captain Blood spoke as if he had read Radar's mind. "Why you? Well it's simple. I only need one hostage and I don't want to waste my energy on the others. They're rather too good fliers or they're slippery customers – unlike yourself."

Radar felt the blood boil in his veins. Captain Blood had singled him out because he thought that he was the feeblest of the bunch, the easiest fruitbat to catch. Well, Radar thought. He'll soon find out differently. This was not the Radar of two days ago. He had out-thought Captain Blood to find a way into his castle and he had managed to save the others inside their dungeon. He also had a little surprise up his sleeve.

As the vampirate approached, he extended his wings to their full extent. Radar felt his heart pounding. This was it, he thought. Just him on his own against Captain Blood. He would pay for all his treachery and his years of terror on the high seas. Radar sucked in his breath, ready to give a garlic-loaded blast. Just a bit closer, a little more, a little … NOW.

Radar filled his lungs and blew.

"That's a present from all the fruitbats," he yelled, waiting for Captain Blood to recoil in horror.

Nothing happened. Captain Blood looked mildly surprised.

"Is that it? Is that your best effort? Did you think you could blow me away when I have sailed through typhoons and withstood enemy broadsides? This is so easy. I had thought you might have something better than that."

"But … but," stuttered Radar. "The … the garlic. It worked on the others, why not…?"

The vampirate laughed. "Oh, ho! So you did have one last trick, after all. Well done. It's just a shame that you didn't know I have no sense of smell. Garlic may frighten off the others, however it has no effect on me. Now come here, my patience is wearing a trifle thin. I will use you as bait to lure your ship closer in. Don't struggle, you little worm."

The vampirate drew his cutlass and pressed

the tip under Radar's chin. "I said that's enough struggling. Got the point?" he hissed.

Radar nodded very slowly. The captain's face creased slightly into an attempt at a smile. "Now to the battlements," he hissed.

Radar looked away from the eyes that were narrow angry slits. At cutlass point he was forced to fly to the battlements. His brain was racing. The captain was going to humiliate him in front of all the fruitbats. If he didn't get away the vampirates would succeed.

At that moment, he emerged on the battlements. He looked down from the wall, saw the chaos in the harbour and then *The Golden Apple*. He could just make out the crew. There were his friends and there was Aunt Bathilda. His spirits drooped. The others had all made it. As usual he had let them down; now he was the bait for Blood's trap.

Just then a cold breeze blew, drying the sweat on Radar's brow and refreshing his mind. Suddenly he felt extra determination run through his body. This was the ultimate test. He had to find a way out somehow. He must not give up. Captain Blood had to have a weakness.

His train of thought was derailed by a loud crash. Flames flickered up into the sky as the vampirates' arsenal crumbled to the ground.

"That's got their attention," hissed Captain Blood, his face glowing in the blood red light. "Ahoy there, you swabs." The deep voice bounced from the rock walls and targeted *The Golden Apple*. "I hope you've brought the treasure chest. Bring it on deck and do it quickly. Otherwise your friend will end up as a lunchtime snack."

Radar could see the fruitbats obeying the orders. The treasure chest was opened. Captain Blood licked his lips at the sight of its glittering contents. It triggered a sudden realization in Radar's brain.

Greed! That was the captain's weakness. He was blinded by his quest for treasure. A faint hope flickered in the back of Radar's mind. Maybe he did have a chance. Radar's hands were shaking as he reached into his pocket and drew out a small, red-velvet box. As if by accident, he let it slip from his grasp. It clattered on to the stone floor.

Captain Blood swung around, tearing his gaze from the treasure chest on *The Golden Apple*. "What's this?" he demanded. "Another trick. Let me see this."

"Oh, please," Radar quavered. "P … please don't take that. I know it's valuable, but it's a family heirloom, it belonged to my grandmother. You're just about to have a chest full of treasure, this small piece won't interest you. Please don't…"

Captain Blood's eyes lit up at the mention of treasure. He picked up the small box. Radar crept forwards so he could almost touch the vampirate.

"You think I should give you this back because I'm about to take all your island's treasure, do you? Well maybe I should, but I won't. I can never have enough gold and jewels. Now, let's see what's in here."

Captain Blood leant his head closer to the box and flicked the catch. The lid flew open and out shot the spider.

"What the … woah!" Taken completely by surprise, the captain staggered backwards. As soon as he did so, Radar sprang into action, giving him a gentle nudge. The vampirate disappeared backwards off the battlements. Radar grabbed the box as it spun in mid-air and took off in one easy move. Not daring to look back, he flew like the wind.

Chapter 12

Nothing was going to stop Radar now. Leaving the burning castle behind, he breezed on to the deck of *The Golden Apple* to cheers and looks of amazement. His feet had hardly touched deck before the ship swung around and began heading out of the cave at full sail.

"I saw it but I don't believe it," breathed Ace.

"You'd better believe it," retorted Swoop. "I always thought you had it in you. Well done, Radar."

"I'll eat to that," Rocket grinned. "Here, have some fruit flan. I've only taken a small bite."

Radar dropped the fruity crumbs as he was clapped on the back by Loopy.

"I knew you could do it – even if you left it a bit too late for comfort," she grinned. "And you didn't need anyone else's help this time, did you?"

Radar felt about two metres tall. He had succeeded. He had beaten Captain Blood all on his own. But was it safe to relax? They weren't out of the vampirates' cave yet. Radar looked behind him. Flames were visible over the castle's wall casting a red glow on the cave walls. He could see vampirates flying to and fro with buckets. Down in the docks, they had their hands full too, trying to save *The Black Fang* from the thick smoke billowing from its hold and rigging. Radar smiled and breathed a sigh of relief. Surely they were safe now.

"Uh, oh, here comes trouble," warned Swoop. "Look! Up in that turret!"

Binoculars and spy-glasses were handed out. Radar focused on the tower at the top of the castle. Captain Blood leapt into focus almost making Radar drop the telescope. The vampirate's face was even paler than usual, he was white with anger. His furious shouts reverberated through the cave.

"You fools, if I can't have your treasure, no one shall. I will have my revenge, even if I don't get the lovely gold and jewels. I will send you all to Davy Jones' locker, you swabs. You won't get away with tricking me."

What was the captain talking about? *The Golden Apple* was nearly clear of the cave, how could they be stopped? Radar glued his eye to the telescope and gulped. He realized what the vampirate was doing. He had forgotten about the Avenger!

He watched horror-struck as Captain Blood lit the fuse of the huge cannon. He stared down the enormous, yawning barrel. It was like looking down a black hole that was about to swallow them all up. Radar's heart sank. In the end the vampirate had beaten them.

There was no time to abandon ship.

"Hit the deck," he yelled, diving for cover.

BANG. Flame spat from the cannon. Rocks and stones whistled through the air, throwing up huge spouts of water when they hurtled into the sea. *The Golden Apple* swayed and rocked as if it was being slapped by a giant hand. The fruitbats clung on to anything solid. Then, to their surprise, the ship righted itself.

Radar opened his eyes. He touched his wings, his legs, his arms. He was all in one piece – so was the rest of the ship and the crew – but Castle Blood wasn't! Radar could hardly believe what he was seeing. Captain Blood was standing amongst the remains of his tower, covered in soot and with his clothes in tatters. He looked as if he had been barbecued. His great cannon had blown itself up. It was split along the barrel. How had that happened?

Loopy broke the silence. Winking at Ace, she said, "I wondered where I put that bumper pack of bubble gum?"

"It certainly was careless to leave it lying around," grinned Ace. "I think it gummed up the captain's plans."

At that moment, a hush descended on the crew. Aunt Bathilda steamed into view.

"Well, I hope the pair of you are proud of yourselves. I want to know what you intended to prove by flying here? What have you to say for yourself, young lady?"

For the first time even Loopy was at a loss for words. She looked appealingly at Radar. People didn't normally ask him for help, but he could certainly get used to it. He stepped forwards, clearing his throat.

"Um, er ... Aunt Bathilda. Why did we come...? Oh ... that's a good question but our trip here wasn't for fun. Loopy was getting some background material for her history project on castles and I was conducting a domestic science survey on the effects of your mystery cooking ingredient. And I, er … I have come to the conclusion that it is an absolute winner – for fruitbats. I think everyone should eat it, a clove a day keeps the vampirates away."

Aunt Bathilda remained motionless. She did not move or speak for minutes. As the seconds ticked away, the fruitbats looked at each other worriedly. Then at last, Aunt Bathilda smiled.

"Do you mean it?" she asked. "Are you saying my cooking's a success?"

Radar thought he had better nod. Once he did so, Aunt Bathilda gave him a huge hug and almost skipped to the bridge of the ship.

"Hurry up there," she shouted. "Full sail ahead. I can't wait to get home and start cooking again."

"Oh, no, what have you done?" groaned Rocket. "This is the end."

"Oh, no it isn't," grinned Radar. "This is

just the start. We've got a whole new lot of adventures to look forward to with the Fruit Gang back together again."

Ace cleared his throat. "And I'm pleased to announce even better news. We have got a new member, if she'll join."

"I wondered when you'd ask!" Loopy crossed her arms and chewed gum for a few seconds, just to make the others sweat. "Of course I'll join," she grinned. "As long as I never hear any more of that nonsense about rules and regulations. You've got six weeks left of my holiday not to mention them."

"OK, OK," agreed Ace and Rocket with a smile.

"Hold on a second." The urgency in Radar's voice quietened the crew. They turned to look at him. Was there something else? What had they overlooked? "You know something? It's extraordinary, I'd forgotten all about it. I can hardly believe it – my flu's gone."

A loud cheer rang through *The Golden Apple*. The Fruit Gang did a fly-past followed by a victory roll as the ship sailed for home, laughter ringing out over the sea…

A few leagues away, a large figure stood immobile. The only sign of life was two enormous fangs that glinted when they moved. Captain Blood hissed under his breath.

"You fruitbats have destroyed my plans, my castle, my beautiful cannon, but you have not seen the last of me. Soon your world will be in ruins too. You will never be safe as long as I live. That treasure is mine! When you least expect me, I'll be back."

With that, the captain wrapped his cape around him and was swallowed up by blackness. Only his words were left as they were caught on the wind and scattered over the sea.